CHOOSE
Us

ALSO BY CAYLIE MARCOE

Parting Chances

CHOOSE
Us

CAYLIE MARCOE

First Printing: April 2014
Cover design by Lisa Hubert

CHOOSE
Us

CAYLIE MARCOE

First Printing: April 2014
Cover design by Lisa Hubert

To Hales
For rhyming with Cales

Chapter One

"Trav, why are we here so early?" I complained as we hiked up the dirt hill to the starting line. I held my styrofoam cup tightly in my hands, praying no one would jostle me and make the much needed coffee fall out of my hands. I could not be held responsible for what I would be forced to do to them.

"I'm not the one who organized this event. Apparently it was someone who despises you," Travis said with a laugh as he escaped my arm which had come out to smack him and ran up the rest of the hill.

"This is torture! How are you guys this awake?" I groaned when I reached the top and took in the chipper riders milling about.

"Riles, not everyone hates mornings like you do. Plus, it's 9:30. It's not early." Travis winked at me over his shoulder and retrieved his bike from the back wall.

"I hate *you*," I replied to his comment with a glare.

"I'll believe that when you say it with a little more feeling." Travis grinned, patting my cheek like a child before hopping on his bike for his practice round.

Ugh. Why did I ever agree to be his personal assistant after I graduated from college? Not only did I have to wake up at ungodly hours, but I also had to run his errands, field his phone calls, make sure everything ran smoothly at events, and do every other random mundane task he could think of. I wasn't sure it was worth the lack of sleep to hang out with my best friend on a daily basis.

Oh, who am I kidding? I love this freaking job.

Sipping my coffee, I headed to the back wall to stay out of the way and pulled out my phone. Might as well get some work done while I wait for Travis to finish his practice rounds. I scrolled through the few e-mails I had waiting and flagged a few important ones I would need to talk with Travis about. As I finished replying to the last e-mail, my phone vibrated with an incoming text message. I glanced at the screen and saw it was from Travis' mom, Kathy.

> *Mom2: Are you there already?*
> *Me: Yeah. Your son hates me.*
> *Mom2: You know him...perfectionist. :) See you soon!*

Sighing, I slid my phone into my back pocket and glanced up to see if Travis was done practicing yet—he wasn't. Guess I could take this time to find some more coffee and wait for his mom by the back entrance. It's not like he'd even notice I was gone.

Ten minutes later I had a new steaming cup of coffee in my hand and was sitting outside against the building near the back door, waiting on Kathy to arrive. My phone buzzed with an incoming text.

> *Trav: Where'd you go?*
> *Me: Coffee run & waiting for your mom.*
> *Trav: Well....at least you missed my crash.*
> *Me: Shut your face!*
> *Me: Did you hurt yourself?*
> *Trav: No. It's just the stupid grooves in one of the hills. Lots of riders are having issues with it.*

Me: Well make sure you figure it out so you don't crash during finals and really do damage.

Trav: I have. I think.

Me: If you hurt yourself, I'm resigning.

Trav: No you're not. Stop lying. You love me too much.

Me: Is love the word you're using for hate?

Me: Because if it is, then yes...that's very true.

Trav: Woman. You are frustrating.

Me: Does that mean you'll fire me?

Trav: Never.

Me: Damn.

"Riley?" A voice asked from above me. Startled, I looked up and saw Kathy staring down at me with an amused expression on her face.

"Hey Kathy," I said, standing up. "One second." I turned back to my phone.

Me: Your mom is here. See you in a few.

"So, how long were you standing there?" I asked as I followed her into the arena.

"Not long. Figured I'd let you finish your conversation with my son." She chuckled. "So, anything interesting happen before I got here?"

"Sure, if you'd call Travis crashing interesting."

Kathy stopped and turned to face me. "He didn't hurt himself, did he?"

"No." I laughed. I'd had the same reaction. "He says he's fine."

"Let's just hope he stays safe during the finals. Did he figure out what went wrong?" she asked when we approached the starting hill and began the climb to the top.

I couldn't help but chuckle at her comment—it's funny how our thoughts worked the same way.

"He did. He said it was the grooves. I'm sure he and the other guys fixed it." I huffed as I lagged behind her in the climb.

"Good. That's good," she said, preoccupied with an incoming message on her phone.

"Hey, it's about time you showed up. The finals are about to start." Travis appeared out of nowhere, startling me. I jumped and watched helplessly as my cup of coffee fell to the ground.

"No!" I cried staring sadly down at the puddle absorbing into the dirt.

Kathy turned when she heard the commotion and looked between Travis and me, then glanced at the ground. She just shook her head, patted her son on the back and walked back down the hill to secure her spot on the sidelines.

I turned to Travis with a glare and smacked him in the stomach as hard as I could.

"Hey. Whoa," Travis said, backing up while rubbing his stomach. "I didn't do anything Riles. You dropped it all by yourself."

"I just…I don't even…" I couldn't even think a clear thought. I needed the coffee which was now turning into mud. I glanced back up at him. He was standing at a safe distance with his hands in his front pockets and just shrugged at me.

"Ugh. Get over here," I yelled, anxious to get our ritual over with. Usually if I could, I would stay at the top of the start hill and watch from the back as Travis did his run. Today was one of the days I wasn't allowed to stay up here. I'd be watching from the sidelines with his mom, so we needed to complete our ritual early.

Travis stepped close to me and pulled me into a hug.

I hugged him tightly and whispered, "Be calm. Be cool. Be safe." This had been our ritual before each of his events since we were 18 and he was just coming back from a broken leg. I'd said those six words to him, and he grinned and nodded at me before having the run of his life. Since then, it just became second nature to say it before his run. Not that it ever stopped him from getting injured or anything—the boy was accident prone— but it was our thing. One of the many quirks of our fifteen-year friendship.

Travis pulled back from the hug, grinned at me and nodded. "Always, Doll," he said, stepping away from me to get ready for his run.

I turned and headed back down the hill to find his mom—or maybe find some more caffeine. Seriously, how did people function this early?

Kathy was still typing away on her phone when I found her on the sideline. She glanced up as I came up next to her. "You didn't kill him did you? I need to know if I have to cancel his events."

"Ha ha. Very funny. He should have gotten worse than what I gave him." I yawned. The first round of the finals was just about to start, so I was stuck where I was for the next three hours.

There goes my caffeine fix.

For the next hour I sat against the fence and watched rider after rider complete their run. Finally it was Travis' turn, and I looked up at the start line, zeroing in on him. I placed my hands over my eyes, peeking through my fingers. I've never been able to watch his full run before, but I would always sneak glances. As much as I didn't want to know, I had to know how he did. For one, he'd ask me a hundred questions later and want me to help dissect the whole thing, and, for two, I just couldn't *not* watch.

I heard the rumble of the crowd as Travis was announced. Then the buzzer went off and I saw him roll down the hill into the first jump. I closed my fingers unable to watch his first trick, but after the crowd erupted in cheers, I opened my fingers and watched as he landed a backflip.

He makes it look so easy.

Still peering through my fingers, I watched as he flew up the next hill with a slight wobble. He launched into an awkward 360 tailwhip and I stared unblinking while he bailed last minute. My stomach dropped when he pushed his bike away from his body and fell violently on the dirt. He lay unmoving for a second, then quickly rolled over and grabbed his ankle.

My breath rushed out of me, relieved that he was relatively okay. I clambered to my feet while the crowd cheered as Travis stood with the help of another rider and slowly limped to the waiting ambulance.

"You go with him in the ambulance. I'll take the car. Text me the hospital name," Kathy said as we walked towards the waiting ambulance, rambling off the protocol she had come up with years ago.

"You sure I should do that? I can't promise I won't injure him more," I hissed through my teeth. It was bad enough that Travis gave a couple other riders a fist bump and was laughing with them. But it was the ridiculous grin on his face that pissed me off the most. He just didn't care about getting injured. *"It'll heal,"* he always says.

Kathy laughed and pulled me into a side hug. "I don't care what you do—just make sure you yell at him first."

"Oh, don't worry, I plan to."

As we neared the ambulance Kathy took out her phone and dialed her husband before giving me a smile and heading towards the back parking lot. Before she was out of earshot I heard her say into her phone, "Keith, your son injured himself again. I swear he takes after your dad."

Before I could get into the ambulance Travis just hopped into, I was stopped by one of the medics.

"You can't go in there. Family only." She nodded to the ambulance.

I rolled my eyes, tired of having to go through this every time Travis crashed his bike. "I'm Riley Logan—emergency contact."

I waited for her to check the paperwork and confirm that I was indeed the emergency contact. Finally she looked back up at me, "Can you tell me the patient's name and date of birth?"

"Travis Grayson, September 18, 1986," I responded automatically, though I was getting more irritated the longer she kept me out here.

She glanced down at the paperwork in her hand and nodded. "Okay, you can go see him now." She stepped aside so I could climb into the back of the ambulance.

"Hey, Doll," Travis said as I approached. "I stayed safe."

I rolled my eyes, standing at the end of the gurney and out of the way of the medic taking care of Travis. "Yeah, your bike's current condition really supports that statement." I heard Mr. Medic chuckle as he injected Travis with some pain medicine.

"Oh come on, I tucked and rolled after coming off the landing. Seriously Riles, it could have been worse," Travis argued, adjusting himself on the gurney.

I snorted. "I'm not sure what could have been worse than seeing you lying there, looking like you were dead."

Travis smiled lazily up at me. "I could have really been dead." I reached out and smacked him upside the head.

Mr. Medic laughed out loud, and then cleared his throat. "Okay enough of that. He may already have a concussion, and I'm pretty sure he has a broken leg. I don't think he needs any more injuries. Especially from his girlfriend."

"We're not dating," Travis and I said at the same time.

Mr. Medic looked between us. "Could have fooled me."

Travis patted the seat next to the gurney. "Come on Doll, you know you still love me and you always hold my hand on the trips to the hospital…while yelling at me."

"Again, I think you're confusing love with hate here." I glared, but still laughed, taking the seat next to him and holding his outstretched hand. He always became super needy when he was pumped full of pain medicine.

"Ah, see there it is." Travis smirked up at me, his eyes already glazing over as the medicine took hold.

"You know, one day you're going to have to find someone else to do this. I'm not sure how much more I can take," I told him, resting my head back against the wall.

The adrenaline was finally wearing off and he glanced up at me with sleepy eyes. "No one else can put up with my shit. Most girls would be crying in the corner. You're my strong, caring, stubborn Riles." He closed his eyes, the pain medicine working its way quickly through his system. "Plus no … can… …your… place…," Travis muttered as he fell off to sleep.

I glanced over at Mr. Medic. "What hospital are we heading to?"

"St. Mary's," he said while flipping through Travis' paperwork.

"Thanks," I muttered. I pulled out my phone and quickly typed out a text to Kathy, letting her know the name of the hospital.

***

Travis and I had been friends a little over fifteen years now. We met when we were ten and his family moved into the house next to mine. He was an awkwardly tall and gangly ten-year-old. Not that I was much different. I was also awkward, wore glasses which covered most of my face, and was as tomboyish as they came. I guess that's what happens when you grow up with three older brothers.

The first time I talked to him I had just come back from my grandma's birthday party, where I'd been forced to wear a dress. I jumped out of the car in hopes of running into the house to quickly change out of the itchy tulle when I saw him on his bike down the street.

He was popping wheelies and jumping the curb. I had never seen anyone so graceful on a bike. I was entranced. I stood at the curb watching him as my family went into the house. Travis glanced up when he heard our front door slam shut and saw me looking at him. He stared back. He had just the hint of a smirk on his face, when his front wheel rammed into the curb in front of me. He fell off the bike in slow motion, ramming his knee down on the blacktop before tucking and rolling to his back. He lay there not moving. I walked over to him and kicked his leg.

"You dead?" I asked in a small voice. Travis still didn't move. So, I kicked him a little harder in the side.

"Ugh, woman. Stop kicking me!" Travis still had his eyes closed, but he swatted at my leg.

"I'm 10. I'm not a woman," I mumbled.

Travis smirked. "Fine. Stop kicking me, Doll."

"I hate dolls," I said, crossing my arms over my chest and glaring at him.

"But you look like one right now." He squinted up at me. I rolled my eyes and kicked him one more time. This time because he was annoying me. Travis laughed and started to sit up, wincing a little. I finally glanced down at his leg to see a tear in his jeans and a bunch of blood soaking the denim.

"You probably shouldn't look at that," Travis said to me, trying to stand up.

I snorted. "I'm not scared of blood." I told him to stay there while I ran into my house to grab the first-aid kit.

When I got back, Travis was sitting on the sidewalk with his leg out in front of him. I plopped down in the grass beside him, and started yanking items out of the first-aid kit.

"This might hurt," I said as I held up a bottle of peroxide. He just shrugged his shoulders. So I did what any 10-year-old girl would do to a boy—I dumped what was left of the bottle on his wound. Let's just say I have never heard anyone scream as loud as he did that day. It's a wonder why he ever wanted to be my friend after that, but that's exactly what happened. We bonded over his bloody knee — and have been pretty inseparable since.

***

The ambulance came to a stop outside the local hospital and I released Travis' hand as the medic rolled him into the hospital.

Travis startled awake and quickly glanced around. "Riley?!" He continued to look around, his eyes out of focus.

"I'm right here," I told him, walking up to the bed. "I'm pretty sure you have to get some x-rays done. I'll be here filling out your paperwork, okay?"

Travis sighed and sank back down into the bed. He nodded as the nurse wheeled him away.

I looked over at the nurse's desk where Mr. Medic was standing with a clipboard. With heavy feet I made my way over to him. This day had exhausted me—and I desperately needed coffee.

"I take it you're going to fill these out?" he asked me as I approached, holding the clipboard out for me.

"I've filled hundreds of them out already. Why not one more?" I said taking it from him and sinking down in the nearest chair. Clicking the pen open, I got to work on filling in Travis' medical information.

Chapter Two

Kathy banished me to the cafeteria once she showed up. I had wanted to wait for Travis to get done with his x-rays, but she walked in, took one look at me, and declared I needed coffee.

Which, I was completely grateful for; it had been a really long day. And honestly, what good was I just pacing the hallways?

I had decided to stay in the cafeteria longer than needed since I knew his mom would be fawning all over him, and it embarrassed Travis to no end. I'd seen it numerous times, and didn't have it in me to make fun of Travis for blushing when his mom would declare it was sponge bath time. You had to find something to joke about, right?

I took another sip of my coffee, when my phone vibrated in my back pocket. I grabbed it and saw I had a new text from Travis.

Trav: Where are you?
Me: Cafeteria
Trav: You abandoned me!!
Me: Psht. Coffee > you.
Trav: Ouch... and I thought my leg hurt
Me: Haha... what's up? You done?
Trav: Yeah getting discharged right now.
Me: Anything broken?
Trav: Hairline fracture. In a walking boot for a couple weeks.

Me: Well it could have been worse.
Trav: Yeah... we've been there before.
Trav: Bring me some coffee!!!
Me: Sigh... The things I do for you.
Trav: :) Thanks, Doll!!

I grabbed Travis a coffee and headed up to his room and found that Kathy was out of mom mode, and into complete manager mode.

"You will have to put out a statement telling your fans you're okay and only have a hairline fracture. We have to rework your schedule though, so you can heal. No riding on it for at least eight weeks. You really did get out lucky this time, only having to wear a walking boot. Also, have you thought anymore about that offer from the TV show?" Without even giving him a chance to answer, she rambled on. I rolled my eyes and handed Travis his coffee. He smiled up at me gratefully with his left leg propped up on the bed in the boot.

As much as I loved Kathy, she was a bit overbearing in manager mode. I would take her in mom mode any day.

"Mom, seriously, I don't want to do a dating show!"

I choked on my coffee. "A dating show? Excuse me?!"

Travis laughed. "Yeah, some new age sports station wants to try their hand at reality dating. Apparently I was at the top of their list for eligible bachelors."

I couldn't help the snort that escaped. "There are people out there who think you're hot?"

Kathy let out a laugh, and Travis smacked my leg. "I'll have you know, people find me incredibly sexy." He stared up at me under his long eyelashes and gave me his signature grin.

Okay, so he was kind of good looking. He pulled off the "just rolled out of bed" hair very well. And damn it, the guy literally rolled out of bed, ran a hand through his dark brown hair, and went on with his day. He was tall and lean — with just the right amount of muscle, in all the right places. But the best feature on him? His eyes. Those damn green eyes, with a brown sunburst in the middle, could make you fall all over yourself to get a closer look. Not that I would know... but I've seen it firsthand. Girls go crazy over those eyes. So, I guess, if you put it all together, he's pretty hot.

Shit, did I just call Travis hot?! What the hell?

Shaking my head to get the creepy vision of my best friend out of my head, I caught the end of what Kathy was saying.

"You're 26, it's time to settle down and give me grand-babies. Maybe this will help get things moving."

"Mom, seriously, you can't expect me to fall in love on a TV show!" Travis whined.

"Of course I don't," she sighed, "but maybe, just maybe, you will meet someone who you can become serious with. Where else are you going to meet someone? You've been busy since you went pro at 16. You've barely had time to breathe, let alone date. Maybe it's time to put the career on hold, and deal with your personal life."

Kathy did have a point. Since his career started, Travis had never had a girlfriend. He was much too focused to let anything come between him and his bike.

"You have what? Eight weeks for your leg to heal, and then rehab, right?" I waited for Travis' confirmation nod before continuing. "I mean, really, what else are you going to do with your time? And plus, I could really use a break from you — I've been traveling non-stop with you since you started this damn thing. I'm ready for my own bed and catching up on all my TV shows." I grinned at him over my coffee cup.

Travis sighed. "Fine. Okay, I'll do it. On one condition."

Kathy beamed at him. "Whatever you want, honey."

"Riley goes where I go and has input on the girls – and I can discuss anything with her." He gave me that damn smirk again.

All eyes were on me, waiting for a response. I rolled mine and shrugged, "As long as I still get to watch my TV shows."

Kathy clapped her hand excitedly and quickly went back into manager mode.

Crap. What had I just gotten myself into?

Chapter Three

Me: You are so dead.
Trav: If I go down, you go down.

Travis had been released from the hospital, and we were in the SUV on the way to the airport to head home. Thanks to the joys of modern technology, Travis and I could have this conversation without his mom hearing from the front seat.

Right after I agreed to... whatever I had agreed to, Kathy jumped into the details that she clearly had been holding back. And apparently, from the start, it was clear I was always supposed to be part of this – whether I agreed to it or not.

Me: Seriously, I have to hang out with these random girls?
Trav: That's the plan, how else am I supposed to get inside details?
Me: TRAVIS – I don't get along with girls! I will probably smack them all before the day is over!
Trav: Sweet, chick fight! Hope I get to watch.

I looked over at him and rolled my eyes. He grinned and started to laugh. "It'll be fun Riles. I get to hang out with hot girls all day — and you get to use your girly-sense to tell me who isn't good."

"Girly-sense? Really Trav?" I groaned. "I can guarantee I won't like any of the girls. And since when do you ever listen to what I have to say?" I crossed my arms over my chest and sighed for effect, then turned my body to watch the city fly by.

"Kids — stop the arguing," Kathy said from the front seat as she turned to look at us. "You both know you would never do anything without each other. It's been that way since you first met. Riley, you know Travis holds your opinion near to his heart, even if he doesn't always *listen* to you." I glanced over at Travis who gave me the biggest toothy smile he could. I couldn't help but laugh at him and relax a little.

"Fine," I said. "I'll do what is asked from me. But seriously, if a girl is a complete bitch, she's out, yeah?" I looked back out the window, relieved to see the airport in the distance. I definitely needed to breathe and step away from this situation for a bit.

"That's why you're here, Riles. You'll be my inside line to the girls. I mean, you'll be living with them, so you'll know everything that goes on behind my back."

I whipped my head back around to Travis, causing a crick in my neck. "Shit." I started to rub the pain away as I looked between Travis and his mom. "What did you say? You said I would be *living* with the girls?" They nodded. "But... that would mean....."

Travis cleared his throat. "The only way I even agreed to do this is if I have an insider. I'm not just going to do it for the heck of dating women. If I do it, I want the best person for me. Not some person putting on a front."

I just couldn't wrap my head around it. I stared, mouth open at Travis — waiting for him to tell me I was being punked. Haha, this was all just a "Let's get Riley really good" game. I mean, he couldn't actually think I would be willing to put myself on TV, in front of millions of people—and pretend I was trying to win his heart. He couldn't be that stupid. This was just crazy.

"I think we need to go back to the hospital. You clearly hit your head harder than we thought." I started to reach forward to tap the driver on his shoulder and give him instructions to get us to the nearest hospital.

Travis reached out and grabbed my arm. "Riles, I know this is not an ideal situation…"

"Travis, no. No, I am not doing this! I did not agree to *this*!" I was shaking my head. "No. Not happening. Nope. Find a new best friend to do this for you." Travis started laughing, and I glared at him. "So glad you find this humorous."

"Riles, it's not like you have to do much of anything. Just lay low, get to know the girls. I'll keep you around until, I don't know, until the top five. By then we should have a feel for the girls, know who isn't fake."

"I just… Travis!!" I whined. I stuck my lip out in an attempt to pout, which I knew did nothing to him – but I had to give it a try. Travis ignored me, like usual, and started gathering his belongings as we had just pulled into the airport parking lot.

"Riles, this is happening. You can either be happy and enjoy the adventure, or you can be a downer and hate every moment. Regardless, you're doing it." He grinned at me as he hobbled out of the car.

I grabbed up my purse and followed him out. "You're saying I don't have a say in this? I'm 25 years old – I'm an adult. I have a say!" I yelled, causing people to stop and stare at us.

"Riles, you made a pact." He turned to face me, crossing his arms and giving me a smirk.

Crap, I was hoping he wouldn't bring that up. We were 16 – and he had just gone pro. We made a pact to never leave the other behind in what we did. That meant go wherever, do whatever, even if the other didn't want to do it. And we had. I went on every tour Travis did. He went along with me whenever I wanted to see a concert he didn't care for, or every other activity I wanted to do when we had down time. He never once bailed or broke the pact, so I couldn't either.

"Fine." I sighed, knowing I had no choice. "I'll do this with you." Travis pumped his fist in the air in victory. "But know, if you even attempt to kiss me, I'll knee you so hard."

Travis laughed and slung his arm around my shoulder. We walked, well hobbled, to the terminal as Kathy chattered away about even more details of what we would be going through, what we needed to sign, and most importantly, for me to try and stay under the radar as much as possible so the other girls wouldn't figure out who I am.

"That seems like a tough feat. If these girls know anything about Travis, they would know I'm with him all the time. There are so many pictures of us out there."

"We're banking on the fact that the girls are just in this for my incredibly sexy good looks."

Great. Not only was I going to have to pretend I was trying to win Travis' heart. I also had to deal with a bunch of girls who were there for the most superficial thing.

It was going to be a long summer.

Chapter Four

We landed back home in Wisconsin and as soon as I stepped out of the plane, I breathed in the fresh air.

"It's good to be home," I said to Travis, who was doing the same as me.

We had been traveling on tour for the last three months with no breaks. Traveling from one big city to the next, over and over and over again… I missed my apartment. I missed my family. But really, I missed home—I missed Wisconsin. It was abnormally cold here for the beginning of May, so I pulled my hoodie over my head and puffed out a breath of air. I could see snow piles littering the ground around the airport. Always expect the unexpected with the weather in these parts.

"It's May and there is snow on the ground! This is all sorts of ridiculous!" Travis yelled out to no one in particular.

"Not like it's the first time," I mumbled as I grabbed my bag and headed to the car.

I threw my bag into the trunk and slid into the passenger seat. It was so nice to be out of the service cars for a change. And I'm sure Travis loved being back in his car. Judging by the huge grin on his face as he slid behind the steering wheel—I knew we were taking the long way home.

"Where to?" He glanced at me before putting the car in drive.

"Just drive," I told him, leaning my head back against the headrest. I closed my eyes and thought over what had been talked about on the flight.

Kathy had come up with a list of things we should and shouldn't do, before and during the show. The first thing was getting someone on all the photos and articles posted about the two of us. Any of the girls that were trying out for the show would probably Google Travis like crazy, and the producers didn't want them to know who I was.

It was amazing how quickly someone could hack systems and completely delete any existence of Travis and me. It actually made me quite sad when I thought about it for long. I mean, our whole friendship was documented online—and now it was just gone.

The second thing was separating Travis and me, so no new pictures would leak. Which meant as soon as Travis dropped me off at my apartment, I wouldn't see him again until we "met" on the show. As if that wasn't bad enough, we weren't allowed to call, text or e-mail each other either. Complete cold turkey. Thankfully the show was supposed to start filming in two weeks, which wasn't too long to be separated. I hoped.

The last time Travis and I'd had no communication with each other was when I was 12, and my family went on vacation. It was before cell phones and internet in every hotel. Even then, I had still sent him a postcard daily.

I really wasn't sure how we were going to manage a communication cut off for two weeks, but if we wanted the show to go smoothly, it was going to have to happen.

The third, and final thing, was changing my past a bit. I obviously couldn't be from the same place as Travis, especially since we came from such a small hometown. I'd be from a town about an hour away—one which had no connection to our hometown. I also had to come up with a career. Clearly I couldn't be Travis' personal assistant.

Everyone was relying on me to not slip up, to not let some odd bit of information through that would let the other girls know who I really was. Guess it was a good thing I had two weeks to myself to get my story straight.

The only good thing about all of this—the producers wanted America to know who I was. They felt it would add a different angle to the show. So anytime I was completely alone with Travis I was able to be his best friend again, we could talk normally, and I didn't have to be coy with telling him who I thought should go. I guess that would make things easier.

Sighing, I opened my eyes as the car slowed to a stop. I had never had such conflicting emotions when staring up at the small two-story apartment I called home.

I was so excited to dive into my bed and pull the down comforter over my head. Yet, I knew this was the moment I'd been dreading since exiting the plane. This was the moment I had to say goodbye to my best friend for two weeks.

I looked over at Travis who was looking at my apartment much the same as I had.

"Hey, I'll see you in two weeks. We'll both be so busy; it'll just fly by," I said, nudging him in the shoulder.

He glanced over at me and grinned, though this grin had much more sadness in it. "Yeah, two weeks will fly by. Don't become all girly on me, okay?" He was trying to lighten the mood and it sort of worked.

I snorted and quickly covered my mouth.

"You just snorted!" Travis laughed.

I shook my head, still covering my mouth. "I don't snort!" I mumbled from behind my hand.

Travis just shook his head and leaned over to my seat. "I'll see you in two weeks," he said, in a low voice before wrapping his arms around me.

I hugged him back hard, blinking back the tears that had formed. When he released me, I gave him the biggest smile I could muster.

"Well, you better go home and rest up. You'll need every ounce of energy you have when you get thrust into a house with fifteen single women." The last part came out of my mouth dripping with sarcasm. I opened the car door before he could see my eye roll and walked to the back of the car, tapping on the trunk. It popped open and I grabbed my bags and started walking to my apartment. I turned around and watched Travis back out of the parking space.

"See you in two weeks!" I yelled toward him. He smiled and waved, before pulling out of the parking lot.

***

I had settled into a routine since getting home a week ago. That meant lounging around my apartment, drinking coffee, catching up on my TV shows and reading lots and lots of articles about Travis' bachelor show. They were calling it *Xtreme Bachelor* and holy crap if the girls weren't all over it. I read comment after comment about how Travis was so hot, and how any girl would be lucky to be on the show. A few of the comments made me want to find the girl and punch her in the face, since it was all "Ohmygod, I would die if I had the chance to date someone so rich and famous! I would never have to work again if he picked me!" I guess these were the types of girls I was supposed to look out for.

Money hungry hussies.

I was hoping the producers would weed the completely superficial girls out, but knew a few would probably be let through. You know, for the drama and ratings and all.

Overall, I couldn't believe how bored I was. I had to fill out my personal profile for the show—the one which would be put on the website for everyone to see. Writing about a fake you is not as fun as it may sound.

Honestly, coming up with a career was pretty easy. Since the questionnaire wasn't asking specific details about where you worked, just occupation, I was able to put personal assistant down without elaborating. If one of the girls were to ask, I would say I was a PA for my dad's construction company, Logan & Sons. No one would know any different.

I also had to deal with dress fittings for the 'first meeting.' Thankfully, since this was a sports-themed bachelor show, I only had to wear a formal dress for the first meeting. For any of the elimination shows, we were able to wear whatever we wanted — which for me would be jeans, a comfy worn t-shirt, probably a hoodie and some Converse sneakers or flip flops. I knew I was going to stand out since the other girls *really were* trying to get Travis' attention and would probably be dolled up from head to toe. But that just wasn't me. And since I'd already had to change so much about myself, my clothes and comfort were two things I wasn't going to budge on.

Chapter Five

I smoothed my hands down my dress, trying to stop them from getting clammy. I had been sitting in the back of the town car for over an hour watching on the little TV screen as all the other women met Travis.

What had I gotten myself into?

I looked down at the dress I had thought was so fancy when I'd first seen it. That was before I had seen all these other women. My dress was simple compared to theirs. It was an olive green one-shoulder dress with draped layers and a hi-lo hem. My auburn hair was left down in loose curls, and I had minimal makeup on—just enough to make my green eyes pop. When I had looked in the mirror before leaving, I couldn't believe the girl looking back at me.

Usually I wear jeans and a semi-loose fitting t-shirt or hoodie that covered most of my curves. Whenever I look in the mirror, I don't see the gorgeous hourglass figure my mom raves about. No, I see athletic legs that are just short enough to make regular length jeans touch the ground, but long enough to make short jeans hit my ankles. I also see wide hips, a soft stomach and a large chest. I have been called pretty plenty of times, and I know I'm extra critical of myself, but all I see is an average girl.

But tonight when I looked in the mirror, I saw the girl my mom always says I am. My legs felt miles longer with the modest two-inch heels I wore. The fabric of the dress draped my body so you could see all the curves of my figure. Never in a million years would gorgeous be a word I would describe myself as. Tonight, it was exactly how I felt.

I had been kind of excited about the whole meeting, but now, after seeing all the other women, in gowns dripping with jewels, I had lost that excitement. I felt like I was the plain frumpy girl again.

To make matters worse, I was the last to "meet" Travis. So I got to see each one of the women flirt with Travis and I got to see Travis' reaction to them. Which was basically him drooling over each of the women. He had a permanent grin on his face and I was getting annoyed. I knew Travis was going to enjoy himself being surrounded by fifteen single women (well, fourteen, since counting me would be ridiculous), but him getting all googly-eyed at them was driving me crazy! How was I supposed to pretend to pique his interest after all of this?

I wiped my hands, which were now completely clammy on the seat. Just one more car and then it was go time. I knew the reason my heart started beating faster was because of the camera crew. It was because once I stepped out of the safe haven of this car, there was no turning back. My nervousness had nothing to do with seeing Travis, or him seeing me all dolled up. Of course it didn't. After all, this was all make-believe on our parts.

I watched the TV as the next woman exited her car. She was tall, thin, had her long platinum blond hair pulled up in a tall, sleek ponytail. She was wearing a super tight and short sparkling gold, sleeveless dress. The camera zoomed in on her steely ice blue eyes as she zoned in on Travis. She quickly made her way up to Travis and pretended to trip, causing her to fall into his arms. I rolled my eyes at her tactics. You could clearly see she tripped over nothing. She giggled, still in Travis' arms, and reached up to squeeze his bicep.

Oh my gosh, could this girl get any more obvious?

Travis had the biggest grin on his face, but I wasn't sure if that was because she had fallen into his arms, or because her breasts were falling out of her too-tight dress. I clenched my hands into fists, forcing myself to breathe in and out, trying to calm myself. This girl needed to go right away. The fakeness was dripping off her, and I could clearly tell Travis had no idea. He was much too interested in her lady assets.

She giggled again, before leaning in to hug him and give him a kiss on the cheek, and then she slowly walked into the house.

Sighing, I slowly drank in a breath, soothing my nerves. My car pulled in front of the house and the driver quickly got out to open my door.

No more waiting, it was go time. The door opened and I accepted the driver's outstretched hand. I stepped out of the car and breathed in the fresh air, before walking towards Travis. I couldn't bring myself to look up as I made my way toward him. This all felt too real now.

Before I could stop myself, I glanced up and caught Travis' eye. He was staring at me, mouth agape. I gave him a shy smile and shrugged my shoulders slightly. Travis slowly shifted his mouth into a dazzling smile, which had me completely forgetting about the cameras that lined the driveway. Travis was wearing a well-tailored charcoal gray suit. He had a white dress shirt on, with thin gray strips you wouldn't even notice, unless you were standing next to him. His tie was striped diagonally in all shades of green. And with Travis being Travis, he was wearing a pair of gray Converse shoes, well okay, one shoe, since he had a walking boot on the other foot. His usual bed head hair was slightly styled with some gel that now made it look casually tousled.

Damn it all to hell if he didn't look hot.

Travis glanced at the producer who gave him a slight nod and turned back to me with the huge grin still on his face and quickly scooped me up in his arms.

"Riles, gosh I've missed you!" he breathed into my hair. Sighing against him, I wrapped my arms around him and hugged him as tightly as I could.

"Can we never do the whole two week break again?" I mumbled into his chest. Travis started laughing and loosened his grip on me allowing me to step back.

"Oh, and by the way - could you stop drooling over every girl that pushes her boobs in your face?" I whacked him in the gut before he could respond.

"Ow. Damn. I can't help it if they willingly put them there!" He was massaging his gut as if I really did any damage. Please, I think my hand hurt more than his stomach did. I was about to mention this to him, but by then, the producer was twirling his finger in the air, telling us it was time to wrap the introductions up.

"Well, I guess I'll see you inside." I leaned up to give him another hug.

Before I could pull away, he whispered in my ear. "I told you to not get all girly on me." I laughed, backed out of his arms, and gave him a wink before walking towards the house.

Chapter Six

When I entered the three-story house that would be my home for the next few weeks, I was immediately met by a waiter handing me a glass of champagne. I gratefully took a sip and entered the living room. One side of the room was completely covered in windows that looked out into the backyard and pool, where there were currently hundreds of white twinkle lights strewn from tree to tree. Beyond the pool, you could just make out Lake Michigan in the dark. I'm sure the view would be stunning in the daylight.

I glanced around the rest of the room. On one side I saw a floor to ceiling river rock fireplace, flanked by two overstuffed loveseats. On the other side was a lavish wet bar, and completing the room were two huge sectional sofas in the middle. They could sit at least fifteen people comfortably.

Taking one more look around the room, I could tell that cliques had already been formed. Standing over by the bar were five women dripping in jewels, including Miss Giggle Boobs. Standing closely off to the side of the group was another bunch of four, who clearly looked like the first, but not as covered in crap. So I'm assuming they were their lackeys.

Note to self: make sure Travis gets rid of those nine first.

Sitting on the sofa were the last five women, each easily mingling with everyone else. They all looked gorgeous, but you could tell it was more in a refined way and not the over the top glam the fakies had.

I made my way over to the group on the couch. They looked up as I approached.

"Oh, hi! You must be the last girl, right? I'm Taylor, it's so nice to meet you!" A woman with long chocolate brown hair and striking blue eyes gave me a genuine toothy smile as she stood up to give me a hug. She was classically beautiful, not needing loads of makeup to make her look like something she wasn't.

Stunned, I gave Taylor a small pat on the back, not sure what to make of her. "I'm Riley." There was a chorus of greetings from the other four girls on the couch.

"Come, sit. Let me introduce you to the others," Taylor said, tugging on my hand.

I let her lead me to the couch to sit next to her. She quickly made introductions for the other women around her. "This is Bethany, Chloe, Erin, and Addison," Taylor said, quickly pointing around the group.

She went through the introductions so quickly I couldn't remember who was who. I hoped this whole thing was just as overwhelming for them too, so when I asked for their names again, they wouldn't mind.

"Where are you from?" The woman I think was Erin asked.

"I'm from central Wisconsin," I said as casually as I could.

"Isn't Travis from central Wisconsin? Do you know him?" Chloe, I think, squealed.

I shook my head. "Wisconsin is a lot bigger than you probably think. With tons of small towns scattered around. I've never run into Travis."

"Oh, that's too bad." Chloe sighed, "You could have given us the inside scoop on him."

I gulped down the rest of my champagne, glancing nervously around the room. "So, where are you ladies from? What's your story? Why did you decide to come on this show?" I guess there wasn't a better time to get the scoop on some of the girls.

"I'm from Oregon," Taylor spoke first. "I'm a software engineer. And a group of my friends decided they wanted to try out for the show, and I got dragged along with. To appease them, I signed up too. Much to their dismay, I got chosen and they didn't. After I had found out a little more information on Travis, I started to get excited about the show." Taylor shrugged. "I figured why not. What do I have to lose?"

"I'm from Vermont, where I work as a dental hygienist," Erin said. "If you can believe it, my mom sent me the information to sign up. I think she wants me to find someone."

"I'm Addison, if you missed that the first time." The girl next to Erin smiled up at me. Her hair was black and cut in a pixie style, which she pulled off perfectly as she peered up at me with her chocolate brown eyes. "I'm a paralegal from Des Moines. Honestly, I just got out of a serious relationship and was just looking for something to take my mind off of it."

Before any of the other girls could introduce themselves, Miss Giggle Boobs spoke up from the bar. "Oh, how cute. We're getting to know each other. What about me? I'm from Chicago. I don't see a need for a job when I can live off Daddy's money. And I signed up, because Travis is hot and famous, and I know I'll have no issue hooking him."

The room fell silent. Before I could come up with something to say back to her, all heads turned to the entryway, where Travis was standing. By the smile on his face, I'm going to say he hadn't heard a word she'd said.

"Good evening ladies. It's so nice to meet all of you," he said, giving them his signature smirk.

"Oh my God, he's so freaking hot!" Bethany sighed under her breath. I couldn't help but roll my eyes and turn my attention back to Travis.

"So, the game plan for tonight is to chat with each of you individually. By the end of the night, five of you will be heading home." A few of the girls gasped.

"Five of us, already?!" Chloe whispered worriedly.

I scanned the room while Travis walked up to the group by the bar and pulled one of the girls away. I had a feeling my chat with him would be the last, so maybe I could let him know who should leave.

"I've met Travis before. He was in Chicago for an event last year. He ended up at the same bar I was at, and he bought me so many drinks. We talked for hours!" Miss Giggle Boobs loudly announced to anyone within hearing distance.

I shook my head at her antics. Not only had Travis probably never met her before, I can guarantee he was never at the bar. For one, Travis never went out after an event. He went back to his hotel and slept. *Maybe* he would go out the next night, if we were still in the city. But I always went with him, and it wasn't to party. It was just to go out, relax and have a few drinks. So, unless this happened when we were 15—and I had yet to start traveling with him—Miss Giggle Boobs was a lying, dirty tramp.

"Oh, you're so lucky, Nicki! I wish I had the chance to meet him before." One of her lackeys squealed.

So Miss Giggle Boobs had a name—a name that was now at the top of my mental list. I didn't care who else Travis sent home tonight, but Nicki better be number one on the list. And Travis better listen to me, instead of making the decision using his 'lower' brain.

Erin left with Travis, as I settled further back into the couch. Girls were still scattered in groups around the room, but the excitement level had lowered as we were reaching the end of the chats.

As I predicted, I was going last, right after Erin came back. I couldn't wait to talk to Travis again. I had to keep reminding myself I couldn't talk to him like I usually do in front of the girls. Times like these, I really wished we had come up with code words.

"He is so nice!" Taylor gushed, sinking into the couch next to me.

"He seems like a good guy, from what you see on TV," I replied lazily. It was getting late, and I probably had one too many glasses of champagne. It was just so hard to say no when there is a seemingly endless supply of glasses coming your way. Plus, with the stupid chatter of the queen bees, I needed something to take the edge off.

"He's also really funny. I think we just laughed the whole time. I hope that's a good sign, I really don't want to leave already." Taylor grabbed two glasses of champagne off the tray the waiter offered her and handed one to me.

"You'll be fine. There are other girls who *need* to go home tonight." I took a big unlady-like gulp of my drink. I knew I shouldn't be drinking more, but I had been on edge since I got into the town car earlier this evening.

"They could all be different people when they are alone with Travis though. He may be superficial and only go by physical appearance." Taylor was eying the girls clustered around the fireplace.

"Don't worry, I'll talk to him about them," I slurred. "Definitely the first to go."

Taylor eyed me. "What do you mean, you'll talk to him?"

Crap.

I slowly leaned forward and set the half full glass of champagne on the coffee table. "I just meant…" I stumbled for something to say. "I mean, maybe I'll mention what Nicki had said. I, for one, do not believe a word that comes out of her mouth. Then he'll find out how much of a liar she is, and kick her out right away," I rambled.

Taylor was still giving me a funny look, so I excused myself from the situation. "I think I need a glass of water." I rushed to the bar to pour myself one.

Note to self: Don't drink so much. You need to think clearly for this. You can't afford to slip up, and that was a close call.

I sipped on the water, slowly making my way back to Taylor, when Erin and Travis came back inside from their chat.

"Riley?" Travis smiled at me. "You ready?" I smiled and headed to the door he was holding open.

The fresh air sobered me up as we stepped outside. It had gotten a little chilly out since I had arrived, but I didn't worry about that for long, because Travis lead me over to a small fire pit, surrounded by three large loveseat gliders. I sat in the one Travis lead us to, and was surprised by how comfortable they were. I kicked off my heels and pulled my feet under myself.

I rolled my glass of water between my hands, waiting for Travis to say something.

"How have you been enjoying yourself so far?" he asked while staring up at the stars.

I took his lead and leaned my head back against the cushion, staring up at the night sky. "I've had too many glasses of champagne." I laughed. "I'm pretty sure they have an endless supply."

Travis laughed loudly, interrupting the quiet of the night. "Only you would get trashed on champagne the first night here."

Yeah, only me.

And Travis knew all too well what champagne does to me.

"Not everyone can have your alcohol tolerance." I flicked some of the condensation from my glass at him.

He started laughing, "Riles, the last time you had champagne, I found you curled up by the toilet."

"I was 16! It was the first time I ever had champagne. And, well, the last."

"That was a great New Year's Eve." Travis grinned.

"Sure it was… for you. You aren't the one who embarrassed yourself in front of your best friend's grandparents. It's a wonder Nana and Papa still talk to me!" I groaned, throwing my head back against the cushion.

"Well, you shouldn't have yelled for the whole neighborhood to hear that your New Year's resolution was to get laid!" Travis was laughing so hard he had tears in his eyes.

Ugh, I hated that he remembered that night, and I only have foggy images.

"Thanks, now that you've embarrassed me in front of America, can we get on with the reason I'm even here in the first place?" I asked, feeling slightly annoyed that my past was being aired like dirty laundry.

Travis wiped his eyes, "So, what did you put down as your job?"

"I'm a personal assistant for my father's company," I replied automatically.

Travis smiled, hearing my made up career for the first time. "It must be hard being a personal assistant. You probably get bossed around, get sent on mundane errands, and probably don't get told how helpful you really are."

I smiled at him over my glass of water, catching the twinkle in his eyes. "You have no idea."

"So, are you getting along with the other girls?"

"Well, I can't say I've talked to them all, so I can't give you a complete honest opinion. The ones I did talk to seemed nice." I rattled off the names of the girls from the couch. "There are a few who seemed to form a clique already, and Nicki, their 'leader' seems a little... She seems over-the-top." I hoped that was enough to say without seeming like I'm pushing him to dismiss someone.

"Cliques? Leaders? What is this, high school?" Travis asked.

"Tell me about it. But that's how it is in there. Nicki mentioned she had met you once before." I casually explained.

"Did she? She never mentioned it when we spoke. When did she say she met me?" He gave me a questioning glance.

"She said it was sometime last year, in Chicago. I guess after an event you went to a bar and she was there. You bought her drinks, talked for hours!" I exclaimed dramatically.

I glanced up at Travis and saw the super confused look on his face.

I knew I was right. Lying dirty tramp.

"I don't really recall that happening, but I'm a busy guy and I've hit my head a few times," he said with a grin.

"Believe me, I know. I've been there every time you hit that big ol' noggin of yours."

We talked for several more minutes, about nothing at all really. I wanted desperately to tell him who I thought should go, but I didn't want to come off to America as a judgmental bitch. I was still me after all, and as much as I didn't want to be on the show, I still wanted America to like me—at least a little. This whole thing was going to be harder than I thought.

Chapter Seven

When Travis and I returned to the house, he was pulled away to a different room to make his final decision. So I secured a seat by the fireplace where I could eavesdrop on Nicki and her crew.

"I just know we hit it off. There is no way I'm going home tonight," one of Nicki's posse exclaimed. I glanced up quickly, and noticed Nicki roll her eyes.

"We have so much in common," Nicki said loudly for the whole room to hear. "I swear he was about to kiss me before the crew said our time was up."

Yep, now it was my turn to roll my eyes at her. I don't think she had ever told the truth in her life. Before I could say something, Taylor came swooping in and sat next to me.

"Don't give in to her. She just wants the attention," she whispered, glancing back at Nicki.

"She is so frustrating! Why would anyone think it's okay for her to be on this show?"

"I'm sure it's the drama she'll add. Helps with the ratings and all." Taylor wiggled her eyebrows.

I couldn't help but laugh. "Yeah, you're probably right. I just wish it would have been anyone but her to add the drama."

Taylor snorted over her cup of water. "Oh sweetie, I think everyone in this room thinks the same thing."

"Even her minions?" I glanced at Nicki, who was swarmed by the other girls.

Taylor barked out a laugh and quickly covered her mouth when everyone looked her way. "Especially her minions. Who do you think is going to get the most air time? Those who lay under the radar or those who make such a fuss about everything and cause the most drama? And right now, those girls know they have no chance of competing against her in the high-maintenance department so they won't get as much air time. They are secretly hoping for her demise," Taylor whispered the last part wickedly to me.

My goodness, I did not realize this TV show would be so complicated. I figured it would be quick, simple and painless. Travis would figure out who was his best fit quickly, and the rest would just be a bunch of fun relaxing time. Guess that's what I get for never paying attention to any of those other dating shows before.

Before I could do anything but stare stupidly at Taylor, Travis came walking back into the room with Tessa, the middle aged retired snowboarder and host of the show.

"Alright ladies, now is the time you all have been dreading. Travis has come to his decision, and five of you will be leaving us shortly. If you could all come and stand in front of the doors, we'll get started." Tessa informed us. She gestured for us all to line up in front of the doors that led to the backyard. The camera crew spent a few minutes positioning everyone in just the right spots before they motioned for Travis to take it away.

"I know I haven't gotten to know you all very well. This elimination is, unfortunately, based on first impressions more than anything. I know it sucks being the first girls to leave, and I very well could be making the wrong choices here, but again, it's all based on the little I have learned about each of you. Sometimes you feel that click and sometimes you don't." Travis was poised, glancing at every girl as he talked, so he wasn't singling just one out.

I tried not to laugh at how professionally lame he sounded. This was definitely a Travis I didn't know. I wondered just how much input the producers were having in what he said or how he presented himself. I hoped it was just for this initial show, and they'd let Travis be himself after this. Nothing like him being a puppet on their strings. I sighed and tuned back into what Travis was saying.

"So, we have these string bracelets you will get if I ask you to stay. You can wear them for as long or as little as you'd like. It isn't necessary to wear them the entire time you are here if you don't want to. It's just my gift to you for continuing this journey with me." He held up the bracelet for us to get a good look at. It was maroon, with two thin strings and what looked like about ten small gold metal beads lining the front. It looked to be adjustable by just pulling the strands in the back.

"So, let's start, shall we? Travis, who is the first person you'd like to stay?" Tessa clapped her hands and ushered Travis to begin.

"This person seemed slightly shy when talking to me, but I am really interested in getting to know her more." Travis played with the bracelet. "So this bracelet is going to Taylor."

I beamed when he said her name. If I could pick anyone right now, it would be Taylor.

She giggled and made her way up to Travis. He slipped the bracelet on her and gave her a hug before she turned around to head back to her spot with a huge grin on her face.

"I can't believe she got picked first. She is so lame." Nicki, who was standing just to my left, hissed under her breath. I'm pretty sure I'm the only one who heard her, but wished like hell the cameras were able to pick up on what she said, so everyone else would know what a bitch she really was.

Travis picked up another bracelet and continued to call girls up to receive them. Erin and Addison were called up, as well as Nicki's wannabe minions Lena, Kara and Holly.

"The next woman was very interesting to talk to and fell all over herself when we first met." Travis grinned while playing with the bracelet.

I let out a low gasp, while Nicki let out a low squeal.

"Nicki, this one is for you." Travis held out the bracelet as Nicki pushed her way past the girl in front of her. She threw her arms around Travis before he could put the bracelet on her and she gave him a kiss on the cheek.

The tops of Travis' cheeks turned slightly pink. No one else would even notice the tinge, but I did and knew exactly what it meant—he was embarrassed from her reaction. I just shook my head slightly at her over dramatic display of affection and groaned inwardly that Travis had kept her here.

Nicki walked back up to her spot next to me with a smug grin on her face. "Sure feels nice to have this thing," she muttered, just loud enough for me to hear. "Too bad you won't know what this feels like."

Ugh, I so wanted to punch her in the face. I wondered if that would be okay, if it would add to the drama the producers were so eager to have.

"Next up, this woman made a quiet, yet breathtaking entrance. She is someone I feel I can talk to about anything, and one who I would love to keep around for a while." He glanced up and made direct eye contact with me. "Riley, it's yours."

I couldn't help the grin that formed on my face as I held my head high and walked past Nicki to receive the bracelet. Travis slid it on and winked at me before wrapping me in a hug.

"Tonight, meet me at the guest house, midnight. Take the door off the kitchen and follow the pathway to the left," he whispered in my ear.

I nodded against his neck then released him and headed back to my spot, with a perma-grin on my face. I glanced at Nicki who was eying me and lifted my arm to acknowledge the bracelet. Nicki scowled at me before turning her body away in the opposite direction.

Krista and Whitney, the last two of Nicki's minions, got the final bracelets, leaving Bethany, Chloe and three girls I didn't know without one.

"The ladies who didn't get a bracelet, I am sorry to say I just didn't feel the click and, unfortunately, your time here has ended," Travis said uneasily.

Chloe burst into tears as she walked up to give Travis a hug, making him even more uncomfortable.

"But we barely got to talk! How are you sure we didn't click?!" she wailed.

Bethany draped her arm around Chloe and led her out the door before she could make a bigger spectacle out of herself.

When all the goodbyes were said, Tessa clapped her hands again, "Well, you've all made it past the first cut! I would suggest you get to bed early tonight since it'll be an early morning for you all. Lots of fun events going on! So, say goodnight to Travis and head on up to bed."

"It's only 10 o'clock. Who goes to bed at ten?" Nicki moaned from the front of the group.

"I do." Travis smiled at her. "I'm exhausted after meeting you all today!"

Nicki melted at his words, "Well, I guess a little extra beauty sleep never hurt."

After we had said our good-nights to Travis and each other, we all headed up to find our rooms. Each room had one of our names on the door. The crew must have done it right after the eliminations.

I found my room on the second floor, and my suitcase was already on my bed. Another thing the crew must have done. I closed the door and leaned back, relieved to have my first completely alone time since this afternoon. No cameras, no crew, no other girls… just me, my thoughts, and this huge gorgeous room.

One wall was half taken up by a window with a huge, comfortable window seat. On the other wall sat a huge queen four-poster bed that was covered with a white quilt with lime green flowers. The wall opposite the window had a small walk-through closet, which entered into a private bath.

I quickly unpacked my belongings and grabbed some comfy yoga pants with a soft cotton t-shirt and headed to the bathroom to take a quick shower.

I stood under the waterfall spray of the shower for much longer than I anticipated, washing off the day's events and thinking over what Travis had said when he gave me the bracelet.

Breathtaking. He said breathtaking. What in the world did that mean? Sighing, I turned off the shower and quickly dried off. I threw on my pajamas and crawled on my bed to relax until it was time to head out to visit Travis. I glanced at the clock. 11:15. Still about 30 minutes before I would need to leave.

I started playing with the bracelet on my wrist. I figured I would take it off as soon as I reached my room. But it was simple and comfortable, and something I would definitely wear in my normal life anyway. There was something else that kept me from taking it off, but I just couldn't put my finger on what.

Chapter Eight

At 11:45 I quietly shut the door to my room and made my way to the servants' staircase, which was located right next to my room. The house was quiet, but I still walked as slowly as I could, glancing down the stairway before I descended, making sure it was clear. Who knew if one of the girls had the case of the midnight munchies?

The bottom of the stairs opened into the dark kitchen. The light of the moon barely made it through the windows, but it was enough to light my way to the door so I could get there without bumping into anything.

I found the door unlocked and quietly opened it, stepping out into the cool night. Closing the door behind me, I followed the path to the left as Travis had instructed.

The guest house was about a quarter mile down the path. It was hidden from the main house by a patch of trees but had the same views of the lake. The house looked small and cozy after being in the mansion.

I walked to the front door and lifted my hand to knock, but it flew open before I could make contact.

"I thought you were going to bail!" Travis pulled me into the house and gave me a hug.

"I haven't had a normal conversation with you in two weeks. You really think I was just going to stay in my amazingly comfy bed and get some much needed sleep?" I mumbled into his chest.

I felt his laugh rumble through him before I heard him. "Well, if it makes you feel any better, I have a pretty comfy bed here."

"Oh thank goodness!" I sighed against him. "I'm exhausted!"

I kicked off my running shoes by the door and followed Travis through the entryway/kitchen area, down the hall and into his bedroom.

That little punk had a king size bed in here.

Seriously, what would one person need a king size bed for? I walked over to the bed and face planted into it, sinking a good inch in.

I lifted myself up on my elbows. "You've been holding out on me. This bed is so much more amazing than mine!"

Travis laughed from his side of the bed, before climbing in and adjusting the pillows behind him.

I rolled to my back and sat up, scooting myself close to him against the headboard.

Damn, even the pillows are amazing.

"I'm never leaving this bed." I sighed, relaxing into the pillows.

"I'm not sure that's what the producers were going for. But it could be arranged." Travis wiggled his eyebrows at me while flicking on the TV with the remote.

I would have hit him, but I felt much too relaxed to even lift a finger.

Travis flicked through the channels at warp speed, twice, before deciding to shut the television off. He threw the remote on the nightstand and leaned back deeper into the pillows next to me.

"Travis."

"Hmm?"

"Why on Earth did you keep Nicki here?" I watched him closely for his reaction.

He groaned and rolled to face me. "I know what you said about her and I was going to send her home tonight. But then I walked out and saw her there and…."

"You thought with your dick. That's what you're saying." I flicked him on his nose.

"Can you blame me?"

"Yes! She is a horrible, wretched, utterly fake woman!" I watched him squirm at my words. "Seriously Travis, I thought I was here to help you make decisions. To tell you who the girls are behind your back. If you wanted to just think with little Travis, then why am I here?"

Travis shook his head and pressed his palms to his eyes. "I know, I know. I messed up, okay?"

I huffed a long breath out through my nose and closed my eyes. I tried to focus on anything other than the stupid decisions Travis made.

"Look, I'll take your opinion into more consideration next time, okay?" He placed a gentle hand under my chin, forcing me to look him in the eye.

"I guess that's all I can ask for." I sighed as I closed my eyes and snuggled deeper into the pillow. "But, if you feel like letting me go earlier than planned, I'd be okay with it."

"Not a chance. You're stuck with me." Travis laughed. He pulled the blankets out from under our bodies and covered us with them.

"Don't let me fall asleep here. I'm pretty sure that would cause major issues if the girls found out." I sank deeper into the pillows. I finally felt completely relaxed for the first time in weeks.

"Mmmhmm, that would be bad." He agreed.

Those were the last words I heard him say before I fell off into a dreamless sleep.

***

"Riles. Riles wake up!" My shoulder was being shaken so hard I thought it was going to dislocate.

"Mmm, five more minutes." I groaned, rolling to get out of the horrible grasp.

"Riles, you don't have five minutes! It's 7:30. You need to get up and get back to the house!" This time I recognized Travis as the shoulder nudging culprit.

"Trav, go away." I threw my arm out, hitting him in the jaw.

"Doll, I can't go away when I have to be at the house in an hour!"

Wait, did he say an hour?

I shot up, rubbing my eyes against the bright light streaming through his bedroom windows.

Shit, I had fallen asleep in his bed. Now I had to find some way to sneak back into the house, with all the girls awake. Double shit.

"Trav, you weren't supposed to let me fall asleep!" I whined, crawling out of bed. "How am I supposed to get back into the house undetected?" I walked over to his windows, throwing my hair up into a messy bun at the top of my head.

I peeked through his curtains and could see the main house just through the trees. People were moving about throughout the house. I turned to the other window which looked directly out to the pool.

"Nice view you have here." My voice dripped with sarcasm. I could make out two figures drinking coffee out on the patio.

Crap, getting back there under the radar was going to be next to impossible.

"Trav, how am I going to get back there?" Groaning, I followed him into his kitchen.

"I don't know. I uh…" Travis glanced around the kitchen trying to come up with a plan. His eyes landed on something and he broke into a smile. "That's it."

I looked down to what he was staring at and laughed. "My shoes? What genius plan did you come up with using my shoes?"

"You went for a morning run. You can go out my back door. There is a pathway that leads to the beach and isn't seen from the house. You can run back up to the house on the beach. No one would know!" He was getting super excited about this plan, except there was one major flaw.

"Travis, I don't run. You know this!" My arms were flailing wildly around, trying to make a point.

"The old Riley Logan didn't run. The new Riley Logan, who all these girls know, does." He popped that damn cocky grin on his face.

"I just want you to know, I hate you," I mumbled, resigned to putting my shoes on. I really didn't have an option and he knew it. He came up with the best plan we had, and I'd have to follow through.

"If by hate, you mean love. Then yes, yes I know." Travis led me to the back door of the house and opened it, making sure the coast was clear.

I punched him in the arm before heading down the path to the beach.

"If I die from this thing you call running, it's all on you," I yelled lowly over my shoulder. Travis' laugh followed me as I made my way down to the beach.

Okay, I guess running wasn't too horrible. Or, in my case it was jogging. A very slow jog at that. But it wasn't bad; it was actually kind of mind clearing. The cool morning air helped wake me up and calm my nerves. And you couldn't get any better with the view of Lake Michigan. In the distance you could just make out an island, but other than that, it was blue water for as far as the eye could see. The beach itself was a small strip of fine sand. Away from the water, the sand turned into tiny pebbles, then bigger boulders. The boulders sat at the bottom of a relatively small, semi-steep grassy cliff. Steep enough by the main house to need stairs to get to and from the beach, less steep by the guest house where Travis was at, where there was only a walking path. The cliff also blocked the beach from the backyard and main levels of the house, so no prying eyes.

I didn't have to run very far before I came into view of the house. I slowed my jog to a walk and quickly climbed the stairs leading to the backyard. Just as I had thought, there were two girls out on the patio. Taylor and Addison were laughing with each other when I approached.

"Hey Riley! Out for a morning jog?" Addison asked catching sight of me.

I smiled warmly at her and nodded. "No better way to start my day. It's quite beautiful out there."

They both smiled at me as I walked past them, quietly sipping their coffee.

"Would you like to join us?" Taylor asked, gesturing to the additional coffee cups and thermos in front of them.

"Oh, um, thanks, but I should probably go shower and get ready. Don't have much time before Travis is supposed to be here, right?" I grasped the door handle, ready to make a run for it.

"Yeah, that's right. He'll be here in about 45 minutes." Addison glanced at her watch.

"Better get going then!" I smiled at them before opening the door and walking into the house. I rushed up the stairs to my room, closing it quickly behind me and leaning against it.

I felt exhausted now that the adrenaline had worn off, but quickly pulled a pair of jeans and a t-shirt from my dresser before heading into the shower to wash off the sweat and sand from this morning's impromptu run.

Chapter Nine

Forty-five minutes later I was standing in the living room sipping my coffee watching the other women mill about, waiting on Travis.

It was so different seeing everyone in the daylight, in their normal clothes. Some girls wore jeans and t-shirts, some wore sun dresses, and a few wore nice dress pants and blouses. This to me looked ridiculously out of place, but to each their own.

"Good morning ladies, I hope you all slept well last night." Travis stood before us wearing faded jeans that fell on his hips and a plain charcoal gray t-shirt, which fit so close to his body, you could clearly make out how muscular he actually was. On his feet, well foot, he wore his ever-present gray converse sneakers. Other than not being in his pajamas anymore, he looked exactly like he did this morning—his brown hair was carelessly tousled.

His greeting was met with a chorus of responses from the girls. All chipper and excited.

Travis met my eyes and brought his smirk up a bit, knowing just how well I slept last night. I just smiled into my mug, averting my eyes from him.

"I wanted to come by and personally tell you about today's events. There will be two group dates today. One will start as soon as we are done here; the other will be later this evening." The girls let out loud squeals, which caused me to jump and cringe.

Nobody should be that chipper this early in the morning. I don't care if there is a prospect of going on a date with Travis. Being overly chipper is utterly ridiculous. I needed at least two more cups of coffee before I could deal with this.

I took the last sip of coffee in my cup and groaned. I couldn't just leave the room when Travis was up there talking to get a refill from the kitchen, but I also knew I couldn't deal with this whole show unless I had more coffee.

I just hoped Travis knew me well enough to not put me in the group date for this morning. I'd be forced to hurt him if that were the case.

"The girls going on the first date are: Taylor, Nicki, Kara, Holly and Riley." I whipped my head up to give Travis an evil glare.

He laughed.

That bastard laughed at my reaction.

He knows how I am in the morning. He *knows*! And to make matters worse, he put me in a group with Nicki.

I wondered if I could get away with kneeing him. He deserved it.

Travis was saying something to the other group of girls, probably something about the time he'd come and pick them up or whatever. But I was too busy plotting his demise to listen, or care.

"So, the ladies going on the first date, if you want to gather your things, say goodbye or get a refill on coffee." He winked. "We'll be leaving in ten minutes." He said his goodbye's to the other girls and then disappeared.

I ran up the stairs quickly to grab my purse from my room. Then took the kitchen stairs two at a time to get the refill I desperately needed.

I stopped at the bottom step, staring into a smirking Travis' face.

"Thought you would need this." He handed me a to-go cup filled with coffee.

I grabbed it from him, took a drink and sighed. Just the way I liked it, with a good amount of cream and a dash of sugar. He knew me well. Then I punched him in the shoulder and pushed him out of the way.

"What was that for?" He glared at me as he rubbed his shoulder.

"You should know better than to put me in the morning date. And you should know better than to put me with Nicki!" I hissed, keeping it low so the girls wouldn't overhear us, and punched him again.

"Okay, okay!" He backed up with his hands in the air. "I'm sorry I put your date in the morning. But I don't have a say right now as to who is in each group, so for that, you'll have to take it up with Jim." He continued to rub his arm, making sure there was plenty of distance between us.

Jim. Mr. Producer who thought it would make ratings soar to have me on this show in the first place. I didn't like him—not one single bit.

"I'm not apologizing." I walked past him to head into the living room.

"I never dreamed you would." He grabbed his own coffee and waited a few seconds before following behind me.

A few minutes later we were heading out to the awaiting SUV. Travis hopped in the front seat, leaving the girls scrambling to get into the seat right behind him, so they could chat with him. I held back, happily sipping my coffee, waiting for the claws to retract so I could safely get into the backseat. I ended up in the back squeezed between Taylor and Kara.

"Where do you think we're going?" Taylor asked excitedly.

"I honestly have no idea. Who knows what Travis has in store for us." I was afraid though for what he was going to have us do. Or what the *producers* would have us do. I've figured one thing out for sure since I've gotten here yesterday: the producers would do anything for ratings.

"Ladies, I hope you are up for something adventurous today." Travis turned in his seat to talk to us. "Because today you're going to get an inside look at what I do for a living."

I couldn't help my chuckle when I heard Nicki gasp in front of me.

"But we're not dressed for riding bikes," Nicki cried.

I choked on my coffee at her statement. I quickly looked at Travis who paled noticeably and had a hard look on his face. He did not like it when someone referred to his beloved profession as just *riding a bike*. There was so much more to it, and I knew exactly where we were going. We were heading to the indoor BMX park. Huge foam pits, big ramps, long rails—so much to do, so many ways to fall. But luckily for Nicki, there was no dirt, so chances of her getting dirty were pretty slim.

"Don't worry Nicki, there are new outfits there for you all to change into." Travis composed himself and smiled at her.

"Is this going to be safe?" Holly sounded worried.

"You only have to do what you want. Though, I would recommend at least jumping into the foam pit. It's such a thrill." Travis was getting more and more excited about this date. I wondered if he forgot he wasn't going to be able to do anything due to his leg.

"But you won't be able to play with us." I smirked at him, glancing down at his leg.

His face quickly fell, remembering his leg. I could see him thinking, trying to come up with something he could do. As quickly as his face fell, he broke into a smile.

"I can still ride around on my bike, just no tricks. Unfortunately, I can't do the foam pit either, but I'll enjoy watching you all do tricks into it." He winked at me, happy he came up with a plan.

"This kind of sounds like fun," Taylor whispered to me, as Nicki and Holly were asking Travis more questions about 'riding bikes'.

"Jumping in the foam pit is fun. Riding a bike into it while doing any trick is terrifying." I thought back to all the times Travis would drag me along when we were teens. He always wanted me to try to do a trick, and before I could even take my foot off the pedal I would freak out and push the bike away from me. There is just something about flying off the ramp and being suspended midair that makes your heart beat too quickly and all logical thought fly out of your head.

"You've done this before?" Taylor asked curiously.

"What? Oh, yeah. My brothers play around with it and I went with them a few times when I was younger."

Jeez Riley, keep on top of the game here.

"Wow. Well, you'll be ahead of all of us." Taylor sighed. "Maybe you could teach me a few things."

"Of course I can. I'm not any good at it, and even with Travis out of commission, he'd still probably be better at showing you things. But I'll teach you what I know."

"Thanks, it would be so great to get into what Travis does for a living." Taylor stared dreamily out the window. "Look at me, I've only known him for a day and I'm already acting all creepy stalker girl."

I laughed at her comment. "You are by far one of the best girls here. Travis would be lucky to have you."

"Thanks Riley. He would be lucky to have you too." She smiled sincerely at me.

Twenty minutes is a long time to ride in a car when you're cramped between two full grown women. Finally we pulled into the parking lot of the indoor park and I scrambled out of the SUV as quickly as possible.

I set my empty cup on the ground while I stretched my legs and back out. I was mid twist when Nicki paused in front of me.

"Don't try and pretend you're warming up for this. We can all see right through you. I can't wait for you to fall flat on your face," she whispered as she walked by.

Oh, it was *so* on. I was planning on just standing off to the side watching the other girls do their thing. But after her comment, I was ready to show her what exactly I can do. What exactly *Travis* had taught me years ago.

"Are you ladies excited?" Travis clapped his hands as he walked toward the building.

He held the door open for all of us. After I had walked in, disposing of my cup in the nearest trash can, I noticed how incredibly quiet it was in the place.

It is never this quiet.

Of course the show would rent out the building. They wouldn't want people to start gossiping about the girls who were still on the show before the first episode even aired.

And if the public were allowed in, Travis would be bombarded and this whole date would be worthless.

"Hello Travis, ladies." An older man appeared from behind the desk. "I'm Dave, the owner of this little joint. Welcome, welcome." He was so cheerful it was hard not to smile at him. He was a tall fit man, with silver gray hair and just the hint of a five o'clock shadow. He still had the look of a rider, muscular legs and arms and a boyish grin.

"Let's get you ladies outfitted, and then Travis can show you the ropes." He clapped Travis on the back, then ushered us into a small locker room.

We each had a gift bag with our names attached. Inside we found a pair of jeans, a black t-shirt with a bright pink *Dave's Bike Shop & Park* logo, and a pair of sneakers.

"Oh my god, could these clothes get any gaudier?" Nicki complained, holding up the t-shirt pinched between her index finger and thumb, like it was a smelly old sock.

"I love this shirt! It's so comfy, and the colors are great!" Taylor pulled the shirt over her head. It fell to just below her hips, but the fit was perfect on her.

Nicki just scowled at Taylor and turned to complain to Holly, who was looking at the clothes with equal disgust.

What was it with these girls? Jeans and a t-shirt are staple clothing in Travis' life. Did they think if they started to date him, they would never once go to one of his events? Or stand next to him when he won an event?

I chuckled at the mental image I had of their heels sinking into the dirt. I couldn't contain the laughter when I imagined Nicki toppling over in the dirt when her heels got stuck. Oh, that would be priceless. Nicki glared in my direction, huffed and grabbed her bag before heading into the corner to change. Obviously she wasn't going to end up by Travis' side, so I would never be able to see it happen in real life. But the mental images were still fun.

Chapter Ten

We headed out of the locker room once we were all dressed in our new clothes and found Travis sitting on a bike near the foam pit. Dave stood just off to his right chatting with him, and they both looked up as we walked toward them, looking like a unified girl band.

"Ladies, I'm glad the clothes fit. If you'll follow me, we'll get you on some bikes so you can start to have some fun!" Dave announced as he led our group over to a back room with rows of bikes. Once we found bikes that fit us, with the help of Dave, and were outfitted with some helmets. Which Nicki complained non-stop about. Then we headed back out to Travis.

"Oh, this is going to be fun." Travis grinned when he saw us rolling our bikes out. He had us start with a few warm up laps around the building to get used to the bikes.

"I haven't ridden a bike in years!" Taylor exclaimed riding up beside me.

I smiled over at her. She was having the best day it seemed and she was game for anything. That is something Travis needed in a girl.

"I know. This is such a fun date!" I giggled next to her. I was having a great day too, regardless of the camera crew around us, and the fact Nicki and Holly were being Debbie Downers. We were only about a half hour into the date and they had complained about everything we'd done. I couldn't wait to see what they had to say when Travis made them jump into the foam pit.

After a few more laps, Travis led the group over to the pit.

"I know you guys are probably not very excited about this. But I promise you, you will have a blast." He got off his bike and walked to the edge of the pit and looked in. He backed up a smidgen, turned and grinned at us, then turned and did a somersault into the pit.

I heard a few of the girls squeal as I stood with a grin on my face. Seeing Travis doing what he loved made my heart soar, though I hoped he didn't land awkwardly and mess up his ankle even more. Travis popped up from the foam with the biggest smile on his face—he looked like a little boy on Christmas morning. He found his way to the ladder and pulled himself out.

"See, nothing to it." He bowed as the girls clapped for him.

"Can I try?" Taylor asked staring wide-eyed at the pit.

Travis grinned, "It's all yours."

"Should I just jump in or do something else?" She was starting to get nervous.

"You can run and just jump in. Once you do that, you can try other things if you want." Travis stood to the side and held his arm out allowing her to go.

Taylor walked back a little way from the pit and glanced around at us.

"You can do it, Taylor!" I cheered, giving her a thumbs up.

She smiled, took a breath and broke into a run. She ran to the edge of the pit and leaped in squealing the whole way. She landed with a bounce and lay in the pit giggling hysterically.

"That was *so much fun!*" she said breathlessly as she rolled and made her way to the ladder where Travis was waiting for her. He helped her out and scooped her into a hug.

"You were amazing!" He squeezed her tight.

"Okay, I'll do it," Nicki huffed, breaking Travis and Taylor apart. Nicki backed up to a line drawn on the floor and took off running. She forgot to jump and did a belly flop into the pit.

I couldn't help it, I laughed, along with Taylor and Kara. Travis had the look of holding his laugh back while Holly ran over to the edge of the pit, got on her knees and peered over the edge.

"Nicki, are you okay?" Holly said on the verge of tears.

"I hate this! This is so dumb!" Nicki sounded from inside the pit.

Travis went to the ladder to help a flailing Nicki out. She clung to Travis when she got steady on both feet.

"You were supposed to jump." Travis smiled while patting her lightly on the back.

Nicki stuck out her lip and pouted even more. "I could have gotten hurt!"

"But you didn't." Travis calmly reassured her. "Look, if you don't want to do this anymore, you can have a seat over there." He pointed to a row of seats just behind the pit.

"Will you sit with me?" Nicki batted her eyes at him.

"I'll come and visit you after the rest of the girls have had their turn here." Travis led Nicki to the chairs, with Nicki complaining the whole way about being by herself.

"I can't believe her. She is just trying to suck up all of Travis' attention. She probably did that on purpose," Kara whispered to me.

I stared at Kara with her short dirty blond bob and honey eyes. She was gorgeous when she smiled, but looked super bitchy when she frowned. I guess I had the wrong impression of her when I first saw her. She obviously was not a Nicki wannabe. Maybe she knew how to play this game better than I thought.

"Well, why don't you show her what Travis likes?" I motioned for her to jump in the pit.

Kara smiled at me and walked to the line. Everyone watched as she took off running and made the jump.

"Oh, that was a blast!" She scrambled out with Travis' help. He was all smiles again.

"I think I'm going to sit with Nicki," Holly said softly, walking over to a scowling Nicki.

"Riley, your turn." Travis walked over to me. "Don't go showing off," he whispered in my ear. I smiled up at him and readied myself.

I had been jumping into these foam pits for as long as I could remember. Travis first took me with him to a park when we were 13 and had me jumping, leaping and somersaulting into the pit by the end of the day. Since then Travis had built one in his backyard and we got to jump into it all summer long. Of course, he would be practicing new tricks into it, while I just attempted to advance my tricks from the edge.

I wasn't going to use this moment to show off in front of the girls. I had nothing to prove to Travis, and I wanted to keep the girls talking to me for as long as I could.

Well, except Nicki. She can stop talking to me anytime now.

I pushed off into a run and jumped into the pit, making sure to bend and separate my knees just a bit to make it the safest landing possible—another thing Travis taught me. I landed with a thump and took a moment to catch my breath.

What a rush!

I always forget the feeling I get when I'm suspended in the air for that split second, and then the feeling of falling into small cubes of foam. It's a crazy adrenaline rush, and I'd missed it.

I quickly turned and started pushing my way through the blue and gray foam cubes to get to the ladder. I looked up and saw Travis grinning at me over the edge of the pit by the ladder, holding his hand out to help me.

He pulled me into a hug, like he did with every other girl, and whispered in my ear, "I saw the dazzling smile on your face. You love being back in this element. Admit it."

"Of course I loved it, I *always* love it!" I backed out of his hug, unable to wipe the smile off my face.

Just then Dave came out of the back room heading towards us. "If you thought that was fun, you should try jumping off the trampoline into the pit!" He walked over to the other side of the pit and slowly pulled back the covering over a built-in trampoline.

"It's much easier to do any kind of flip into the pit off a trampoline," Travis said, hobbling over to Dave. I caught Travis' grimace when he started walking. He must have hurt something when he jumped in the pit.

Stupid boy never takes care of himself like he should.

I quickly made my way to follow Travis, pulling up beside him when he stopped; I leaned in and quickly whispered before the other girls made their way around the pit, "Don't even think you're going to jump in again. I see your hobble." I pulled away and stepped over to meet up with Taylor and Kara.

"What was that about?" Kara questioned, looking between Travis and me. Travis wore a guilty-stunned look on his face. He glanced over at me with the look of a dare in his eyes, and I minutely shook my head.

"I just asked Travis if I could try this first," I said loudly enough for Travis to hear.

He still looked like he was about to dare me to do something, which was frustrating, because he knows I will never turn a dare down. Lord knows he's tried to get me to back down, but when you grow up with three older brothers, backing out of a dare is not built into your vocabulary.

"Yes, Riley asked to go first. But I want to make this interesting. So, if you're game Riley, I'd like to play a game of dare with you." Travis brought his cocky smile back out.

Damnit! He knew I wouldn't backdown!

"Depends on what it is," I said coyly. I wasn't going to accept right off the bat—even if that's what I was programmed to do—I had to remember the setting we were currently in.

"I'll keep it easy. I dare you to do a backflip into the pit." He cocked his eyebrow and waited for my answer.

A backflip, this was child's play.

"I'm not sure Travis; I wouldn't want to hurt myself," I said through my teeth. What was he doing? Trying to get the girls to hate me?

"I overheard you talking to Taylor earlier. Your *brothers* do a little BMX, and you've tagged along a few times." He just grinned at me.

DAMNIT!

"Okay, fine. I'll accept your stinking dare." I seethed and walked over to the trampoline.

Travis stood back with Taylor and Kara, who had looks of pure fear on their faces. I glanced up to see Nicki laughing with Holly and pointing at me. I'm assuming she was thrilled thinking she was about to see me fail.

Sorry to disappoint you, Nicki.

I started jumping in the middle of the trampoline, trying to get as much air under me as I could. After I was about five feet in the air, I started bouncing myself towards the end of the trampoline nearest the foam pit. I jumped a few more times—keeping the five feet of air under me—before taking a deep breath and launching myself into a backflip. In the few seconds I was completely airborne I fought with my body to do what my mind was telling it. Finally, I got around and made sure I went into the pit feet first.

I landed, exhaling the breath I didn't realize I was holding and fell back into the foam cubes. I heard a squeal, followed by clapping, and looked up to see Taylor, Kara and Travis at the edge of the pit all smiling down at me. I did a little fist pump and started moving toward the ladder. I pulled myself out, right in front of Nicki, who was snarling at me.

"Showoff," she hissed just loud enough for Holly and me to hear.

"At least I'm having fun with Travis, instead of pouting in the corner like a child," I taunted back, before turning my back on her and heading over to the trio on the other side.

"That was awesome, Riley! Can I try?" Taylor asked breathlessly. She looked over at Travis who just shrugged.

"Have you ever done backflips before?" I asked Taylor, since Travis was still just staring at me.

"Well, no. But it looks easy." She started sounding less thrilled to attempt it.

"In that case, I would start with just jumping in off the trampoline. Work your way up. You need to land feet first, or you could get injured. Once you feel comfortable, add some twists and such," I explained this to her as we walked over to the trampoline. Travis was being so useless. This was his stupid group date, why isn't he telling her all this information?

"Okay, I guess that'll be fun too." Taylor tried to hide her disappointment.

"It will be fun. Promise." I patted her shoulder as she walked onto the trampoline.

Travis finally decided to move and came to stand next to me. "Do you have any idea how cute you looked when you were lying in the pit? All smiles and fist pumping," he asked in a low whisper.

I snorted, "Cute, yeah right. Did you bang your head today?"

I could feel Travis staring at me again, so I redirected his attention to Taylor—who was just getting a little air beneath her—by cheering for her. Taylor probably had two feet of air beneath her, when she jumped into the pit screaming. I rushed to the side in time to see her head pop out of the cubes, smiling.

"That was amazing!" she squealed, climbing out of the pit excitedly.

Kara went next, jumping on the trampoline before launching herself straight into the foam.

"Oh man, this is so much fun!" Kara exclaimed, grabbing Travis' hand to get out of the pit.

We went back and forth for the rest of our date, taking turns jumping in the pit, in all sorts of different combinations. By the end of the date, both Taylor and Kara had managed to do a somersault from the trampoline into the pit. And even Holly left Nicki's side for a few minutes to try her hand at jumping in. Nicki just sat on her chair, frowning at us the whole time. The only time she smiled was when Travis went over to talk to her for fifteen minutes. She also couldn't keep her hands off him. And he seemed to be happily soaking it in.

Yes, I saw it all, because I couldn't take my damn eyes off them. I figured it was 'research' for my job on this show… but the more I watched them, the more I wanted to claw Nicki's eyes out and tell her to get her hands off my guy.

Wait a second, my guy? Where did that come from?

I shook my head a little, mentally scolding myself for getting caught up in all this crap and went to join the other girls.

Chapter Eleven

Once again I was stuck in the back of the van, but this time I had a window seat. Which was perfect, since I didn't really want to chat with anyone. I just wanted to stare out the window and try to figure out where that thought had come from. It wasn't like I hadn't seen Travis with other girls before. Sure, he'd never had a steady girlfriend—but there had been a few girls. I usually ignored them. They were typically summer flings. Or maybe more accurately, city flings. And they were all clingy, prissy, annoying girls. They would get upset when Travis would only want to hang out with them in the hotel room watching movies and ordering room service. Every single one wanted to be seen out and about with Travis. They all wanted their fifteen minutes of fame.

I don't know what attracted Travis to those girls. Well, okay, I'm sure I have some idea what attracted him to them. The girls were stupidly gorgeous, and Travis is just a guy after all. They were also all superficial, just like Nicki. It was the exact reason why I agreed to do the show. I didn't want another one of those girls in Travis' life.

He's making it really hard for me.

But even though all the girls were exactly like Nicki, I never once wanted to claw their eyes out. Never once was I…*jealous* of them. This show was definitely getting in my head. It was only day two, and I already needed a break from this. That was the only logical answer to my craziness. Because I was *not* jealous of the other girls hanging out with

Travis. And I did *not* call Travis 'my guy.' That was just absurd.

Sighing, I leaned my head against the window, watching the never ending line of trees pass by. Every so often I caught glimpses of Lake Michigan peeking through. All I wanted to do was get back to the mansion, grab a stiff drink and lounge about in my room for the rest of the day. Travis however, had other plans, when he turned in his seat to talk to us.

"I'm sure you are all starving after our date today. So, we're going to stop at this little burger place by the lake. I hope you all eat meat, because I can't even describe to you how amazing their burgers are," he told us excitedly, rubbing his hand on his belly.

There was a murmur of excitement about the prospect of food, since none of us had eaten since breakfast. And we had been busy jumping around all morning.

I knew where we were going; a 1950s burger joint called Lu-Mick's that has amazing lake views. Nothing has changed since it opened in the 50s, except the prices, which were still reasonable. You can get their signature Mick burger for $1.35. But I wasn't sure if the other girls would be okay with eating delicious thin grilled burger patty, on a grilled hard roll, with cheese, a pat of butter, ketchup, brown mustard and pickles. I swear everything about the burger would make girls like Nicki and Holly scream and run away. Not only do you usually get so messy, because the juices are leaking out of the bun when you take a bite, but the darn burger has a pat of butter on it!

It's freaking amazing.

Oh and the malts?! Ugh, they are so amazing. Smooth, creamy, with just the right amount of malt flavor. Chocolate malts from Lu-Mick's are by far the best malts ever!

We pulled up to the old white building with red trim. A big flashing 'Eat' sign positioned on top of the building, with the vintage Lu-Mick's sign fading just to the right of the door.

"I'm going to order us some burgers, fries and malts. You ladies go secure those tables by the lake," Travis said, motioning to the picnic tables which were lined up on the grassy patch of land behind the building. The picnic tables had blue plastic tablecloths taped on, to keep them from blowing away with the wind gusts coming off the lake.

We pushed two tables together to give us some space while eating and sat down, waiting on Travis and the food.

"This place probably failed the food safety inspection," Nicki complained. "Travis better not expect us to eat that crap."

"Can you imagine how many calories are in that stuff?" Holly bemused as she sat next to Nicki.

"I know. And Travis didn't even ask us what we wanted. He just went to get it. I would rather have a salad," Nicki commented.

I couldn't help the snort that came out of me. "This place does not serve salads. It has served the same food since it opened in 1952. Burgers, fries and malts. That's what you get. And you know, if you actually ran around and had fun at Dave's, you wouldn't be complaining about the calories since you would have burned them all there!" I was frustrated with those two.

"How do you know this?" Nicki questioned me.

"I grew up in Wisconsin, Nicki. Lu-Mick's is a staple for anyone who lives here. Anytime my family would come to this area, we would always stop here." This was actually the truth. Nicki just didn't need to know Travis and his family were always with us whenever we did come.

"I can't believe people eat like this," Nicki scoffed in my direction.

No, she did not.

"Nicki, this is Wisconsin. Home of brats, beer and cheese. What the hell do you think we grew up on?" I yelled at her. "You indulge in moderation! But by no means do you have to eat a freaking salad to remain healthy!" I was standing up at this point leaning over the table getting into Nicki's face. This girl was driving me crazy!

Nicki scanned me up and down. "Yeah, I can see you grew up on that." Then she turned her back on me to whisper something to Holly, who also eyed me and laughed.

I was ready to attack the bitch. I was so close to jumping across the table and putting my fist in her fake face, when I heard a subtle cough from behind me. I regained my composure and turned to see Travis standing there with bags of food in his hands. He walked to the table setting the food down.

"Riley, would you help me bring the malts out?" he asked, lowering his gaze to the ground.

I heard Nicki giggle, before I agreed and we headed back into the restaurant.

No one was in the place, except for the two cooks, who headed to the back when we came in. Our malts were stacked nicely in cardboard holders on the counter. Travis walked up to them and took a seat on one of the bar stools by the counter. He patted the one next to him for me. I begrudgingly walked over and sat.

I heard rustling behind us, and turned to see one of the camera crew had followed us in and positioned themselves in the corner, camera pointed on us.

"What was that about?" Travis asked, staring intently at the malts.

"Nicki is a bitch Travis. She is a horrible woman who has nothing nice to say about anything or anyone," I ground it out through my teeth.

"Do you really know her that well?" He looked up at me this time, with questions in his eyes.

"I don't need to know her! I have known enough people like her to know her kind. Travis, you weren't out there. She basically trashed our upbringing. And she made a snarky comment about my weight!" I was yelling now. I couldn't help it, I was so irritated. Irritated that Nicki was still here, irritated that Travis clearly didn't see her how I saw her. Irritated that I couldn't have this conversation with my best friend off camera.

"Riles, you shouldn't jump to conclusions. This is all new for her. You need to take it easy on all of them; after all, you've only known them for a day," Travis said, staring right over my shoulder.

"Travis!!" I screamed. He jumped back a little, but I continued with my voice raised, "You cannot be serious. You are sticking up for her? You are taking her side in this? Do you even want to know what she said to me? About me?"

Travis just shook his head, "No, I really don't. But the Nicki I have known has been nothing but nice and caring.

She had a rough day today; she probably just wants to go back to the house and rest."

My jaw dropped. Was this really Travis sitting in front of me? I reached out and touched his forehead to make sure he wasn't feverish and out of his mind.

Damn, he felt fine.

"Travis, please tell me you are joking right now," I begged him.

Again he shook his head, "Please just take it easy on her."

"No! No Travis, I won't. You asked me to be here so I could help you pick. So I could see who the girls really are. I'm telling you who Nicki is, and you don't believe me! Hell, you want me to 'give her a chance.' You think she's so great!" I stood up and started pacing in front of the counter. I couldn't look at Travis anymore, I was bound to smack him if I was anywhere near him.

"Yes, that's why you're here. You're my best friend, and your opinion matters to me. And I know you are able to see who the girls are at the house. But what I'm saying is anytime I've seen Nicki she has been nothing but nice to everyone. So, I really think maybe you are the one upsetting her and she's just fighting back," Travis explained, picking up a malt and taking a sip.

"You…wait…what?!" I stammered. I stopped in front of Travis and stared at him until he looked up at me. "Travis, you *always* do this! You always find a girl you think is gorgeous and easy. You have fun with her for a weekend or two and then it's over. You move on to a different city. But this isn't like that anymore. You are on a show to find someone to date. To really *date*! Do you really think I am just going to stand by while Nicki plays you and you fall into her trap? Do you really think Nicki is the one for you? And are you seriously going to tell me, you believe her over me? You believe a woman you've known *one day* over me who you've known fifteen years?!"

"I'm asking you to stop being a stuck up bitch and start giving people who are not like you a chance," he said, glaring at me now, clearly upset that I was not backing down.

I was shocked. Travis called me a bitch. He's never called me a bitch before. I couldn't do this anymore; I stomped over to the door and let out a frustrated scream.

"Don't you dare walk out the door while we're talking." Travis stood.

"Go to hell, Travis." I spit back at him, before leaving the restaurant and heading towards the SUV.

I climbed into the backseat and swiped at the tears that were now streaming down my face. Not only had we gotten into our first ever fight, but he had also managed to make me cry. My heart felt like it was being torn into two and I had a horrible feeling that I was going to lose my best friend over this.

Chapter Twelve

Was I being an overly dramatic fool? Travis and I never fought. I never brought up any issues with the stupid girls he was with. What the hell was going on right now?

I had sat in the SUV until everyone was done eating, sad I wasn't enjoying in the deliciousness that was Lu-Mick's. Even more upset Travis and I had fought over something as dumb as Nicki.

Too much estrogen around me, that had to be it.

I needed to hide out in my room for a while. To get away from these girls, especially Nicki and to figure out what the heck was going on with Travis. I seriously wished I could be around when Travis and Nicki were alone together to see what exactly she was like. Or I wished Travis would just realize I wouldn't lie to him.

I hadn't said a word when the girls came back into the vehicle. Nicki smirked at me, figuring I'd gotten talked to by Travis, and was probably going to be the one going home tonight. Yeah, that's right. The producers decided to do another kick off right away. They figured they would have enough coverage from the two dates and Travis would be able to see which girl still wasn't clicking with him. Only one would go home tonight. Then it would be a weekly thing, with the possibility of the top five getting stretched out to every two weeks. Depended on the ratings and the budget.

I wished it was an elimination every night, so I could be home in a week, but I knew it couldn't happen that way.

Hadn't anyone heard of speed dating?

We pulled into the driveway of the house and I waited very impatiently as Nicki took her ever loving time getting out of the vehicle. As soon as her feet hit the blacktop outside, I rushed out of the SUV and pushed my way past her—literally pushed—causing her to stumble to the side, and mutter a few cuss words under her breath; I could hear them and hopefully so could Travis.

I ran into the house, passing the girls who stayed behind, who were excitedly trying to ask how the date went. I took the stairs two at a time and sprinted down the hall to my room. I threw the door open, slammed it behind me and sank down to the floor against it. I hugged my knees to my chest and placed my head down on them. Pretty much the same position I took whenever Travis got on his bike. I closed my eyes and thought about the last hour and a half. About the argument with Travis. About him taking Nicki's side. About him calling me a bitch.

A single tear slipped out of the corner of my eye, and rolled down my cheek, dripping off the corner of my chin before landing on my jeans. I sniffed and pressed my palms to my eyes, willing the tears that were threatening to stay in. I don't know what had come over me. Why did I care so much about Nicki and Travis? If he wanted to waste his time with her, why should I care so much? Yes, I was brought on this show to help him decide, but sometimes Travis would make his own decisions and not care what I think. Clearly this was going to be one of those times. I should just roll my eyes and walk away… and let him make the biggest mistake of his life. But I couldn't. Even after all the crap he said to me, especially the calling me a bitch part, I still couldn't just walk away from him. I wanted to hate him. To be angry with him for weeks. But that wasn't me. Did I need him to apologize to me? Yes. Did I need to apologize to him? Probably.

Leaning my head back against the door, I took a deep breath. I held it for a few seconds and slowly released it.

What is going on with me?

This just wasn't right. I was stressed and overwhelmed with the TV show, but there was something more that just wasn't right. I felt not only hurt by what Travis said — but... jealous? Was I jealous of Nicki? Was I jealous that Travis clearly had feelings for her?

Psht. No. That couldn't be it.

I needed sleep. Yep, that's what I needed. Maybe if I took a quick nap, I'd wake up feeling refreshed and ready to take on the rest of the day. Maybe I'd wake up to my old self again. Not this crazy, hormonal, over reacting, jealous girl.

No, not jealous. I was not jealous!

I kept telling myself that as I kicked off my shoes and slid under the covers. I snuggled into the pillows closing my eyes. My body relaxed, my breathing evened, and I drifted off to sleep imagining Travis lying next to me.

I woke up to a dark room, with the sound of someone pounding on the door. I looked over at the alarm clock. *8:30, holy shit I slept a long time!* I scrambled out of bed and hurried to the door, since the pounding never stopped. I threw the door open and stood face to face with Jim, the producer.

Jim had to be in his early 50s, his light brown hair had more silver pieces now than brown. He also wore a full beard which was completely silver. His eyes were a soft blue—yet they were currently staring hard at me.

"Riley, you need to get downstairs right now. The elimination was supposed to happen an hour ago," Jim said leaning against the door frame.

I rolled my eyes and leaned back against the door frame opposite of Jim. "I'm not going down there. I'd rather go home right now."

"Don't be so dramatic Riley. You and Travis had a fight. You'll make up and everything will be back to normal." Jim stated, glancing at his watch. "But we really need you to get downstairs, before the other girls start a rally to get you thrown out tonight."

"And what makes you think Travis isn't going to eliminate me tonight anyway?" I asked, curious for his answer.

"Riley, Travis has been moping around all day since your fight. He was the biggest drag on the second date today. I watched the video feed; I saw what happened between you two. But by the way you have both behaved since, I can tell you'll be back to best friends again by the night's end," Jim said pushing me back in my room. "Now, go get changed and get downstairs. I'll go hold them off for a little while longer. The girls currently think you got ill after the date and that's why you came straight up here when you got back." Jim started down the hall before I could respond. As I was closing my door I heard him mumble, "If I didn't know any better, I would swear those two had feelings for each other."

I closed the door and quickly got changed into a new pair of jeans and an old faded football t-shirt. I ran to the bathroom to check my reflection in the mirror. Ugh, dark circles under my eyes, thanks to the makeup I cried off. I washed my face as quickly as I could and assessed the damage again. No more circles, but no more makeup either. I swiped on a quick pass of mascara and some lip balm and called it good. I slipped some black flip flops on my feet, pulled my hair into a messy bun on the top of my head and headed downstairs.

The girls were all situated in front of the wall of windows, just like last elimination. Travis wasn't in the room yet, but Tessa was there, standing next to a table with the bracelets. They were navy blue this time. I twisted the maroon one on my wrist, and noticed Taylor pointing to an open spot between her and Kara. I slowly made my way there, passing a snickering Holly and Nicki.

"I hope you're all packed," Nicki whispered as I went by.

I decided to ignore her. Obviously there wasn't anything I could do that would stop her from acting like a bitch. And Travis was clearly not listening to a word I had to say. Why waste my breath? Why even care anymore?

I found my spot, ignoring both Taylor and Kara who were trying to talk to me and just stared ahead at Tessa. Honestly I didn't care if I got sent home. I actually hoped Travis had gotten sick of me being there and decided he didn't need me here. Okay, well, I didn't wish he would get sick of me, but I did wish he could make this stupid decision by himself. It's not like he even cared what I had to say.

Why was I on this stupid show?!

Travis walked in then. The sleeves on his red and brown plaid button up shirt were rolled up to his elbows, making his muscles very visible.

Stupid him, looking stupidly attractive. Damnit!

"Hello ladies. Another night none of us are looking forward to. But I am glad I got to hang out with you all a lot more today. I hope you all had as much fun on our dates as I did." He greeted us, clapping his hands together.

Everyone, except me, replied with some sort of excited agreement. Yeah, sure, I had a great time—until you decided to pick Nicki's side over mine.

"So based on today's date, I've made my decision on who I would like to keep here and continue to get to know better, and the one person who I just didn't feel that connection with." Travis continued, picking up the first bracelet. "This first bracelet is for the woman who maybe didn't have the best time on our date, but tried to keep a positive attitude."

Oh, come on!

"Nicki, this one is for you." Travis held the bracelet out for her.

She squealed and ran up to him, yet again, just about tackling him into a hug. He put the bracelet on her and leaned in to give her a kiss on the cheek. She walked back to her spot grinning like an idiot. She looked up at me and gave me the same ugly self-righteous smile she always saved just for me.

Travis rattled off a few of the other girls. I was barely listening, but I saw Taylor, Kara, Erin and Addison go up. Also three of Nicki's minions, whom I just didn't care enough about to learn their names, had gotten bracelets.

I finally zoned back into the surroundings and noticed Taylor giving me a sad look.

"What?" I whispered to her.

"It's you and Holly left. I just don't want to see you leave tonight," She whispered back to me.

Of course I was left in the bottom two. I honestly had no idea what Travis was going to do.

"Will Riley and Holly please come up here?" Tessa asked, pointing to the spot right in front of Travis.

I walked forward, noticing two small pieces of tape stuck to the floor where we were to stand. Seriously, did the crew have every move pinned down?

I thought I was going to notice the cameras around all the time, but I barely ever remembered they were there. The only time I caught them was when Travis and I were alone in the restaurant, and that was only because they came in after me. Every other moment the cameras were on me, I usually forgot about them and went about my day.

Wow, I was going to have to remember not to do anything majorly embarrassing.

Travis cleared his throat. "I don't like making this decision. But I'm basing it on what happened on our date. And for that reason, I'd like this bracelet to go to…" He paused, rolling the bracelet between his fingers.

I glanced over at Holly who appeared to be shaking. You could clearly see the tears forming in her eyes. She has been here for one full day! What is it with these girls who think they are in love with Travis after one freaking day?!

Holly choked out a sob and turned to stare at me with tears rolling down her face.

Wait, what just happened?

I turned back to Travis; he was holding the bracelet out to me.

"Riley?" he asked looking slightly confused.

Huh, he called my name.

I walked forward for Travis to put the bracelet on my wrist. He slid it on, running his thumb over the first bracelet. He pulled me into a hug and whispered close to my ear, "Tonight. Get to my place as soon as you can."

He released me and turned to hug Holly and lead her to the door to say goodbye. I turned in a daze and was quickly in the arms of Taylor who gave me a big hug.

"I'm so glad you're still here!" she whispered to me.

I just smiled at her.

"It should be you he's leading out tonight," Nicki hissed brushing past me to go get a drink at the bar.

Again, I didn't say anything to her, but turned back to Taylor. "I'm going to head up to bed. I've just been exhausted."

Taylor nodded, "Yeah, they said you came down with something right before we were going to eat. I hope you feel better." She smiled at me.

I smiled back before heading slowly up the stairs to my room. I collapsed on my bed, not even bothering to kick off my shoes.

Travis wanted me to come to his place. He wanted to talk. I guess that was a step in the right direction, but was I willing to go there? Did I really want to rehash what went down earlier today? I was already exhausted; I didn't need more issues today. My eyes started to feel heavy.

I'll just close them for a few minutes.

Chapter Thirteen

I woke up to the sound of a door slamming somewhere in the house. Everything else was quiet. I realized I was still in the spot I had fallen on my bed in and I tried readjusting myself, pulling myself up by the pillows and getting comfortable.

I closed my eyes, my finger playing with the bracelets on my right wrist. My eyes flew open.

"Travis!" I gasped, rolling over looking at the clock. One a.m.

Oh shit!

I scrambled out of bed, thankful I was still dressed and quickly made my way to the door. I slowly opened it, peeking out to make sure the hallway was clear.

It was dark and silent in the hall as I softly closed the door behind me and made my way to the servants' staircase. I ran down the stairs, avoiding the steps I knew made noises and peered around the corner into the kitchen, which was also dark. I quickly moved to the door and out of it as quietly as I could. I took a few steps away from the house, before turning around to look and see if any lights were on.

Everything was pitch black on this side of the house, so I quickly sprinted to the guest house. As I got close to the house, there was a single light shining from the back of the house. Probably from his bedroom, if I remembered the layout correctly. I reached the front door, ready to knock, but stopped before my fist hit the door. I reached down for the knob and tried to turn it. It was unlocked and opened smoothly. I let myself in, shutting the door slowly behind me and sliding the lock in place. I kicked my shoes off by the door and tiptoed down the hall to his room.

I was able to see Travis sprawled out on his bed before I even got to his room. The light was coming from one of the bedside lamps. As I entered, I heard his heavy breathing, so I knew he was sleeping. I made my way to the bed, and gently kneeled next to Travis. He didn't even stir. I lay down next to him and just took him in. He was on his stomach with his arms under his head. His biceps just peaked out from beneath the sleeves of his white shirt. I reached out and ran my finger down his arm.

Why does he have to be so attractive even when he's sleeping?

He stirred when I touched him, so I brought my hand under my head and watched as he slowly opened his eyes and took in the room. He blinked a little and his eyes focused on me.

"Riles?" He reached out and touched my face softly. "Are you really here?" He had the look of hope in his eyes but his voice sounded broken. It may have even cracked a little.

"Yeah, I'm here. Sorry I'm so late." I closed my eyes as he gently cupped my face with his hand.

"What time is it?" he asked, his voice scruffy from sleep.

"A little after one. I didn't think I was going to fall asleep, so I never set my alarm. But I guess I was more exhausted than I thought," I explained.

He sighed and rolled onto his side facing me. "I thought you weren't going to show up."

"To be honest, I didn't think I was going to either. When you whispered it to me, all I could think was…why?"

I sighed, nestling into the pillow and pulling the covers over me.

"What changed your mind?" His voice lost the scruffiness as he continued to wake up.

I peered at him under my eyelashes and took a deep breath before I answered. "Travis, we have never fought before. Ever. And we've been around each other almost 24/7 for the last five years. Do you realize how uncanny that is? People fight, they argue, it's what happens. And yet, we never did." I noticed Travis give me a slight nod before I continued. "So this fight. This *stupid argument*, caught me off guard. Especially because of what… or who it was about."

"Riles, I'm just out of my element here." Travis started to explain. I reached over and grabbed his hand to stop him.

"Just, let me talk, please?" I pleaded. He just stared at me and started rubbing his thumb up and down my hand.

Taking another deep breath, I continued, "Travis, I agreed to do this stupid TV show with you, because you asked. That is all. You asked and I agreed. You know I would do anything for you. But it was also so I could help you. So I could weed out the girls who are no good for you. If anyone knows who is good for you, it's me." My voice was rising and I could feel the anger start to bubble up again. Travis continued to rub my hand, which had the calming effect I needed to continue. "But it seems you don't want to listen to me, Trav. You seem like you don't even care that I'm here." Travis paused the rubbing and just held my hand.

"Riles, I'm going to talk now, and you're going to listen. First, whatever you think of me not wanting you here—you can wipe that thought right out of your pretty little head." He gently tapped my nose before continuing. "Second thing, yes, I am a dumb guy. Yes, my first instincts are to keep the hot girls here. I've only known them for a day—how much am I supposed to find out about them in a day? Even after the one-on-ones yesterday and the dates today, I still know barely anything about any of the girls. So yes, I'm being stupid when it comes to them. And hell, Riles—I am so freaking sorry for what I said and how I acted today." He dropped my hand and pressed his palms to his eyes.

I couldn't help it. I really wanted to hold the grudge longer than a few hours, but with him clearly on the verge of tears and the crack in his voice, I couldn't take it anymore. I moved closer to him and laid my head on his chest.

"I get it Trav. I probably overreacted more than I should have. Nicki just knows how to press my buttons and it's so aggravating," I whispered into his chest.

His body rumbled with a laugh as he ran his hand up and down my arm, sending chills through my body.

"I'm so, so sorry Riles," Travis whispered, his voice cracking. "I can't go through how I felt today, after the fight, ever again. I love you, Riles."

I found his hand and gave it a squeeze. "I love you too, Trav. I don't ever want to feel that way again either. And I'm sorry too." I took a deep breath and quickly pushed out what I wanted to say. "So, I've decided I'm going to give up on Nicki. Clearly there is too much drama there and I can't stand for it to really come between us again. If you want to keep her here, you can, and I won't say anything. Hell, I will avoid her to the best of my ability. I just hope one day you'll finally see what I see." Travis laughed and pushed my shoulder while I smiled into his chest.

"Well, thank you. I'm glad that drama will be over with." He continued to run his hand up and down my back, which was slowly lulling me to sleep. I could feel his hand starting to slow on my back, but my eyes were too heavy and my body felt too weak to even attempt to move off him.

Just as I started to feel myself drift off to sleep again, I felt Travis lean down and kiss the top of my head, then whisper, "But for the record, if I had to choose, it'll always be you, Riles. Always."

Chapter Fourteen

I woke up bright and early, stretching out under the covers. The sun was just peeking over the horizon, and there was a gentle breeze flowing through the room. It was weird waking up by myself. For the last two weeks, I had slipped out of the main house and spent every night talking with Travis at the guest house. We would chat about the girls for the first 20 minutes, and then move on to everything and anything else we could think of. It felt like the old days, before the show, and I was so glad our argument hadn't ruined our friendship.

Since I had always gone over there so late, we always ended up falling asleep. Which forced me to sneak out of the house and do my stupid morning run down the beach.

Which, okay, let's face it—I was kind of enjoying. The last few days, instead of just running back to the house, I would run the opposite way on the beach until the property line ended. Then I'd run back up to the house. It definitely helped me clear my head and feel less stressed about still being here.

I had kept my promise and avoided Nicki the best I could. But I swear the woman thrived on drama—she always seemed to be searching me out. Which was so ridiculous, and I didn't know why she even bothered, but apparently this was a serious competition to her, and I was her biggest threat.

Travis was actually listening to what I had to say about the girls. There had been another elimination and Travis and

I had talked the whole night before, going over each girl. A few girls really did know how to be a completely different person in front of Travis. Since he wasn't going to kick Nicki to the curb, the next best was someone from her posse. And Travis shocked us all on elimination night when he decided to send two girls home. Jim had tried to step in and explain to Travis the show was on a perfected schedule and changing the eliminations was going to cause issues. But Travis pulled out the "When I signed on, you said I could do whatever I wanted" card. He also mentioned he had no connection to either of the girls so keeping them on was cruel. So, on elimination night, Whitney and Krista, two of Nicki's followers, were the ones to leave.

Nicki had laughed—yes laughed—when Whitney and Krista weren't given an olive green bracelet. Well, okay, so she was standing right next to me and I heard it clearly, but anyone else would probably have thought it was a little cough. I think that was when I figured out Nicki was in this to win it. She had even faked out her supposed friends. She only cared about herself and would do anything to climb to the top. I really hoped Travis would get the hint and kick her out soon.

Something had also happened that the producers never really thought about. One of the girls got homesick and wanted to leave the show. Jim tried to talk to Lena about staying, even offering her a phone so she could call her parents, but Lena had made up her mind and was already packed and ready to leave. This really threw Jim and the other producers into a tailspin. We were now down to six girls in the competition. Jim grumbled that everything was falling apart and now instead of having a show running for ten weeks; it was going to be a five-week show.

Travis had come up with a solution to that issue. Instead of having an elimination weekly, it would be bi-weekly or every three weeks, depending on what Jim felt like doing. This would also let Travis get to know the girls better and there would be more dates added on. Jim was reluctant to agree, but really didn't have much of a choice, considering everything that had happened. When the other girls had found out what was going to happen, they were thrilled. Not only would they not be going home anytime soon, but they would also be hanging out with Travis a lot more—a win-win situation in the girls' books.

Last night Travis said he had some things to go over with the producers about upcoming one-on-one dates. I hadn't wanted to be around the girls after Travis left the house for the night, so I excused myself and hid out in my room. I took a long shower, letting the water rain down on me, relaxing me. Then I curled up in my bed and pulled out my laptop—which I had to keep in my room at all times and not let the girls know about, since they weren't allowed to have any access to the outside world. I had wanted to catch up on some TV shows, but I only watched maybe five minutes before I had fell asleep. I woke up again around three and shut everything down, sliding the laptop back in its case and under my bed, before falling back into a dreamless sleep.

Now, even though I didn't have to sneak anywhere, I got out of bed and threw on a pair of green shorts and a gray tank top. I laced up my running shoes and headed out down to the beach for my morning run. I took my same route, just starting at the main house instead of the guest house. It added about a quarter mile on to the run, making it a complete two mile run today.

Breathing heavily, I slowly took the steps to the backyard and collapsed on the grass, laying on my back and staring up at the blue, cloudless sky. My mind started to wander, thinking about what today's events would be. Travis had mentioned something last night about there being a one-on-one date today. The first individual date of the show. I really didn't care who he took on the date, but I prayed it wasn't Nicki.

When my breaths evened, I picked myself off the grass and headed back to my room to get myself ready for the day. The house was still quiet when I walked in; I glanced at the clock in the hallway and noticed it was just after 6:30.

Wow, I was up early today!

No wonder the house was still quiet.

I closed the door to my room, locking it and heading to the bedside table. I opened the drawer and dug behind the few paperback books that were stacked in front, and pulled out my phone. It was another thing that was banned from the house, but I was able to have. I only looked at it about once or twice a day here—which was amazing, since before the thing was typically attached to my hands every minute.

I slid my finger across the screen to unlock it and saw I had a few new text messages. I opened the first one that was just sent five minutes prior.

> *Mom2: Hey hun! Happy Birthday! Hope you have a fun day!*
> *Mom2: PS. Tell Travis to take it easy on you today. ;)*

Whoa. The show had taken up my entire life and I hadn't paid attention to the date while I was here. It couldn't be May 27th already, could it? I glanced down at the phone, pulling down my menu bar and sure enough May 27 flashed back at me.

How in the world did I forget about my own birthday?!

My phone vibrated with an incoming call, I glanced and the screen and smiled.

"Hi Mom!"

"Happy birthday, honey!" Mom said cheerfully.

"Thanks. I miss you guys."

"Oh, everything is just the same here. Nothing to miss. How is the show?" Mom asked.

"Ugh, you wouldn't believe some of these girls. But overall, it isn't horrible. And I think there are a few real contenders," I said, thinking of Taylor and Kara.

"Well, that's good. I always hoped Travis would end up with a great girl." Mom sighed into the phone, making me feel like she wanted to say something else.

"What is it?" I asked.

"Oh, nothing. Your dad is at work right now. He said he called and left you a message earlier today," Mom continued.

"Yeah, I haven't really had the chance to check my phone today."

"Well, I suppose. I'm sure you have things to do. I hope you have a wonderful day."

"Thanks Mom. I love you and miss you," I said into the phone, feeling like I was about to choke up. I've always had a tight relationship with my parents, even visited them at least once a week for our weekly dinners. The show had put a damper on a lot of things in my life.

"Love you too sweetie. Bye." Mom hung up the phone before I could get any more emotional.

I checked the other three messages, which were all Happy Birthday greetings from other friends and listened to Dad's message—which made me teary eyed—then I scrolled back to Travis' moms messages and read them through again before responding.

Me: *What do you mean, take it easy?!*
Mom2: *Oh….you'll see! ;)*
Me: *Being secretive is not cool!*
Mom2: *You'll have fun, promise! Just don't tell Travis I mentioned anything to you.*
Me: *Ugh!!*
Me: *And thanks. It's weird having my birthday here with a bunch of girls I don't really know.*
Me: *Or like…*
Mom2: *I believe it! But it'll be a great day, I know it!*
Me: *If you say so. I gotta get cleaned up now.*
Mom2: *Okay, I'll talk to you later! Love ya!*
Me: *Love you too. Miss you! Bye!*

With that weird cryptic message in my head, I quickly showered. I spent more time putting on my makeup than I usually did. A little eyeliner, light eye shadow and mascara were basically the most of my makeup regime. I blow dried my hair and styled it into a low loose side ponytail, draping my hair over my shoulder, leaving my side swooped bangs down.

I opened the closet and stared at the contents. T-shirts and sweatshirts, that was what I owned. I saw something peeking out behind one of the t-shirts in the corner and moved all the hangers down. There, in my closet, was a summer dress. The top of the dress was a pale yellow, with random scatters of tiny red flowers. It had a sweetheart neckline and thick sleeveless straps. It was cinched at the waist and fell softly away from the body down to the knees. Halfway down the yellow turned into an upside down V of multicolored flowers, which floated out to create a flower lined border at the bottom of the dress. I reached out and touched the dress, causing a note to flutter to the ground. I scooped it up and read:

Riles, I know you aren't into dresses, but my mom said this would look great on you. And that you should wear it today. I told her she was crazy and you wouldn't do it.. but what do I know?! Put it on. Look girly. I'll see you soon!
-Trav

I smiled down at the note, setting it gently on the table, before walking back to the closet and pulling the dress off the hanger. I walked into the bathroom and slipped into the dress, staring at myself in the mirror.

His mom was always right when it came to clothes, and this dress looked amazing on me. I felt like I did on the first night. Beautiful. It was a simple dress but it hugged my curves just right and hit me just above the knee. The color stood out against my newly bronzed skin—thanks to all those morning runs.

I walked back to the closet to grab some shoes, when I saw a pair of black flip flops with floral pattered fabric straps. I smiled as I slipped into them.

She thought of everything.

Me: Thank you for the dress, it's amazing!
Mom2: Dress? I didn't send you a dress.

Me: Travis said you picked it out...
Mom2: Oh hun, you and Travis are so oblivious.
Me: What is that supposed to mean?!?!?!
Mom2: Nothing.
Me: UGH! You're lucky I have to go downstairs!
Mom2: Have fun!!

Sighing, I shoved the phone back in the nightstand behind the books. I took one more look at myself in the full-length mirror before heading out the door and down to the kitchen, where I grabbed a mug and filled it with coffee and added a large splash of creamer. I took a sip and relaxed against the counter.

"Good morning, Riley!" Taylor bounded into the kitchen looking extra chipper today.

"Mornin'," I mumbled against my mug.

Taylor poured herself a cup of coffee and stood there grinning at me.

"What? Why are you looking at me like that?" I asked while brushing at my face in case I had something on it.

"When were you going to tell me?" She still had that grin on her face.

Wait? What?! How did she know?!

"I...uh...I mean... I didn't know..." I stammered trying to figure out what to say. I glanced over to where the camera crew were hiding out and they all had the same "oh shit" looks on their faces.

"Eek! Happy Birthday!" She flew over to me and trapped me in a hug.

"Oh... Right, my birthday. That's today..." I mumbled patting her on the back looking over her shoulder at the crew who relaxed immensely. "Wait, how did you know it was my birthday?" I asked when Taylor released me.

"There is a huge banner up in the living room." Taylor smiled and led me out to the living room.

I stood, mouth agape, staring at the large banner which said *Happy 26th Birthday, Riley!* Oh, yeah, this was embarrassing.

"What did you do to suck up that much to Travis?" Nicki asked as she walked by us into the living room.

I bit my tongue—literally. Couldn't I just have one day where I didn't have to deal with Nicki? Just one? Right when I was about to break my promise to Travis and put Nicki in her place, I heard a high pitched scream come from the doorway. Erin and Addison flew into the room holding three envelopes in their hands.

"They are here! Group dates and one-on-one date announcements!" Erin squealed.

"Well, open them. I'd like to know if I'm the individual date, so I can go freshen up," Nicki complained from the back of the room.

Freshen up? It was 8:30 in the morning. I just shook my head and turned my attention back to Addison, who was opening the one-on-one date envelope.

Riley,
It's your birthday and we're going to have some fun!
You'd better bring you're A game!
I'll see you at 9 am.
-Travis

The other girls lost their excitement at the mention of my name. And I'm pretty sure I heard Nicki scoff behind me, but really, I didn't care. Travis was taking me on a one-on-one date, and it was my birthday! I didn't have to spend it with people I hardly knew. I got to spend it with my best friend!

I just barely heard the details of the two group dates. One was taking place tomorrow, the other the following day. That meant I could potentially hang out with Travis all day long.

Yeah, this was turning out to be a pretty great birthday!

Chapter Fifteen

At 9:00 I walked out of the house to find Travis' car parked in the driveway. Travis was leaning against it, in his typical outfit and was wearing that damn sexy grin. I glanced back at the house to see if any of the girls were watching us. I couldn't see anyone, and quite frankly at this moment I just didn't care. I took off running to Travis and flew into his open arms.

He hugged me close and kissed the top of my head. "Happy Birthday, Riles."

"Thanks," I said taking a step back, then smacked him on the arm.

"Ow, what was that for?" he asked rubbing the spot I hit.

"Why did you have to go and put a huge stinking banner up for the whole world to see?" I asked getting into the car as he held the door open.

Travis chuckled and closed the door heading over to the driver's side. I took a moment to glance around his car. Two small video cameras were added to each side of the car, pointing at the driver's seat and my seat. I turned to look behind me and noticed for the first time there was an SUV parked behind Travis' car and the camera crew was piling into it. I relaxed just a little at the thought of them not being in the car with us, even though they had cameras on us. I could deal with inanimate objects that recorded me—maybe.

Travis slid into the car and grinned, "So birthday girl, we have a big day ahead of us!" With that he took off down the long driveway.

"Where are we going?" I asked as he turned out of the driveway in the opposite direction from the city.

"What have we done every year for your birthday Riles?" he asked, sneaking a smirk at me.

Oh man. I was not dressed for that!

"Why on earth would you want me to wear this to go mini golfing?" I huffed at him, folding my arms across my chest.

"Two reasons. Number one, I'm hoping it'll deter you from doing awesome." He laughed. "Number two, you look ridiculously hot in it."

"Wha..um… Bu…wha?" I couldn't spit out a single coherent thought. All that was running through my head was: *He called me hot.*

"Yes, I'm so going to win this year!" Travis pumped his fist in the air, smirking.

"Trav, you know, just because you put me in this dress, doesn't mean I still can't kick your butt. Do we need to remember what happened when we first met? Pretty sure I was wearing a dress then." I informed him, making him remember our meeting.

"You didn't kick my butt. I fell off my bike trying to impress you!"

I snorted, "Yeah. Whatever you say. But are you forgetting the part where I had you screaming like a little baby?" I asked feeling a smirk come across my face.

"You dumped a whole bottle of peroxide on my open wound!" he wailed, wincing at the memory.

"Right. I'd call that a victory for dress wearing Riley."

"You are so…," Travis started. "Just…ugh…."

I started laughing. I couldn't help it. Travis always had to have one up on everyone—it's part of the reason why he excels so well in his profession—he's unable to let other people have the victory. Oh yeah, this was going to be a great day!

We pulled into our usual mini golf place, Al's Mini Golf. The first time we came here on my birthday, I had turned eleven. It was the first birthday I celebrated with Travis. We had so much fun that day, when my birthday came around the next year and my mom asked what I wanted to do, I said mini golfing. Eventually, it just became a tradition. And even though I'd been traveling with Travis since he'd gone pro, and my birthday usually fell around an event, we'd always made time to find a mini golf place wherever we were and play a round.

I'm not going to lie; we were competitive. Eventually, our parents and siblings stopped coming with us because we were just too over the top. Travis and I usually went back and forth each year with the winning. Our current scores were: Travis—8, Riley—7. I was bound and determined to bring it back to a tie.

We got out of the car and walked up to the concession/ticket shack. Behind the open window sat the ancient owner of the place. His name was Alfred and he opened this as a small nine-hole course when he was 20. He had to be in his 80s now. The course had been updated throughout the years. He first added another nine holes. Then he added different 18-hole levels. Currently there were a total of 72 holes, four different levels: kids, advanced, difficult and extreme. Alfred tried to update some of the holes yearly so if you are a regular you aren't always playing the same course.

Travis and I always go for extreme. We haven't played here in five years, so I was curious as to what had changed.

Alfred was busy cleaning the golf balls when Travis rang the bell on the counter. Alfred looked up at us, took a moment to register who we were, and then broke into a toothy grin.

"Well well. I see I'm the lucky guy who gets to enjoy your birthday battle this year." He shuffled towards us, pulling out our usual golf clubs and handing us two golf balls, one bright green, the other bright yellow.

"Hey Al, how have you been?" Travis asked, shaking the old man's extended hand.

"Oh you know, I'm not getting any younger." Alfred laughed at his own joke and smiled gleefully at us.

"It's good to be back here. I can't wait to see what has changed," I said to him, with a smile.

"You'll have some fun up there on extreme. I've changed a few holes since you've been here last. I can't wait to see who comes out on top. What's the score now?" Alfred took the money Travis handed him and rang up our game.

"I'm kicking her butt Al!" Travis laughed and grinned like a kid.

"Um, the score is eight to seven. I would not call that kicking my butt." I pushed Travis' shoulder with my own.

"Ah. I'm going to have to cheer for Riley today." Alfred handed us the score card and a little pencil.

Travis' smile fell. "I thought we were friends, Al."

"Oh son, you always cheer for a beautiful woman." Alfred pointed out, giving me a wink.

I'm pretty sure a blush appeared on my cheeks, but I returned Alfred's smile and leaned across the counter to give him a kiss on the cheek.

"Thank you Alfred," I whispered in his ear.

"Oh, and happy birthday sweetie." Alfred gave my shoulder a little squeeze, before releasing me. He looked over my shoulder, "Who are those folks?"

Travis and I turned to see the camera crew standing behind us. We had somehow forgotten about them again.

"They're Travis' posse." I grinned at Alfred. He let out a little laugh and turned to Travis for an explanation.

Travis sighed, "I agreed to do this TV show…" Travis stopped; I'm assuming he was hoping to get off with that, and not have to explain what the TV show was about.

"And this TV show is about?" Alfred asked, causing me to laugh.

"It's a…dating show." Travis rushed out in a mumble.

"What was that? You'll have to speak up son, I'm not as young as I once was," Alfred yelled toward Travis, cupping one hand behind his ear.

Travis sighed again, and spoke louder and slower. "It's a dating show."

"And why are they following you and Riley around right now?" He sounded confused.

"Riley agreed to help me weed through the girls," Travis explained.

Alfred looked between the two of us for a minute before speaking, "Huh. I always figured you two would end up together." He shrugged and turned back to his cleaning. "Have fun out there!" He called out to us as we started climbing the stairs to the extreme course.

"You know, it's not the first time I've heard someone say that." Travis broke the silence we had fallen into as we climbed the stairs.

"Heard what?" I asked, lost in thought.

"Us ending up together. I've heard a few people say that." Travis stopped at the first hole, grabbed my yellow golf ball from my hand, and placed it on the green artificial grass.

"What? Why have you never mentioned this before?" I lined myself up by the ball and mindlessly swung, letting the ball follow the path down to the hole. The ball came to a stop just shy of the hole. But my mind was elsewhere.

"I just, I don't know. I thought it was silly," Travis said stepping up to the green and hitting his ball down the course. His settled right next to mine.

"Huh, us together. That would be just...odd," I muttered walking past him to my golf ball.

"Yeah, odd," he murmured following me down to the hole.

***

We were approaching the eighteenth hole. I was currently losing—by one freaking stroke. To win this year, I had to sink this as a hole-in-one, and of course, it was probably the most difficult hole on the course. Since we had traded off on who went first, it was Travis' turn. He crouched down, setting his ball down on the turf and trying to eye up the hole.

This was one of the holes Alfred had changed. It used to just be a big drop to the hole, where it was all about luck sinking a hole-in-one. This new hole had a semi drop with another hill, then it slightly turned to the right, before dropping down another hill. The hole was on a plane right at the bottom of the last hill, in the center of the green. Of course it was possible to get a hole-in-one, but it would take either all the luck in the world or a lot of strategic planning—which was what Travis was currently doing.

After about two minutes of eyeing the course and making adjustments to the placement of the ball at the starting line, Travis finally stood up and got into position. He adjusted his body slightly and lightly swung the club back and then forward to collide with the ball.

The ball went soaring down the first drop and skipped over the hill, taking a wide right turn around the corner and dropping down the last hill. The ball had gained momentum going down the last hill and flew right to the hole. I held my breath, if Travis got this in one shot, I was screwed. The ball rolled right past the hole and settled next to the edge of the course.

I exhaled and grinned at Travis' frown.

"I still have a chance!" I jumped excitedly toward the starting line.

"Psht, you can't sink this in one shot!" Travis rolled his eyes in my direction, pointing to the difficult course.

I just shrugged my shoulders and turned my back on him. I had studied the course as Travis had been over analyzing his shot and I dropped the ball to my feet, positioning it with my shoe. I had one chance at this, and I just hoped I was right about what I thought I needed to do. Instead of swinging directly down the center, like Travis did, I hit the ball toward the right wall. My ball made the drop and rolled up the hill, hitting the right wall at the top of the hill and following the wall around the curve and down the hill, nowhere near the hole. The ball rolled to the back wall and bounced off it, sending it back into the direction of the hole. The ball had lost momentum when it hit the wall, so it was moving at a snail's pace towards the hole.

Once again, I held my breath watching the yellow ball inch towards the hole. Finally, after what felt like hours, the ball dropped into the hole and I heard the whirl of it as it fell down the pipe and rolled its way back to Alfred in the shack.

I let out a squeal and jumped up and down. "I did it! Woohoo! I beat you!" I turned to Travis with a huge grin on my face.

He didn't look defeated. In fact, he looked happy. Or maybe entranced? He stood there with his sexy grin on as I jumped up and down cheering for myself. I was twirling around, making my dress float out around me, when I felt strong arms circle my waist and lift me off the ground and spin me in a circle. I looked up to see Travis' face inches from mine. He wore a breathtaking smile and just stared down into my eyes. After another spin, he set me on my feet, but didn't release me.

I wasn't sure if my heart was beating too fast because of the excitement of winning, or the fact that I was standing this close to Travis with his arms around me and could smell the mint of his breath. Travis moved one hand from my waist to my face and ran his thumb across my cheek. His other hand was still firmly on my waist and pulled me closer to him.

Tingles flashed through my body at his touch. Which was...odd.

"God you're beautiful." He breathed out causing my heart to escalate.

I couldn't say anything snarky back to him, like I usually would. I couldn't do anything at all except gaze into those green-brown sunburst eyes.

My eyes flicked down to his mouth when I saw him slowly moisten his lips. My body was acting on its own accord and I was slowly leaning up to Travis. I peeked up at him from under my eyelashes and saw his eyes flutter shut. I smiled and let my eyes close too, while my body kept moving towards his.

My mouth was mere centimeters away from his when I heard someone shout, "Always bet on a beautiful woman!"

Travis and I jumped back from each other, and turned toward the shack where Alfred was leaning against the back door, holding my yellow ball in the air. I smiled down at him and took a few deep breaths to try and relax my nerves.

What just happened there?

Travis gave me a look I couldn't place and opened his mouth to say something, before quickly closing it, shaking his head and walking down the path towards the hole to finish off his game.

We tallied up the scores and I won by one stroke, bringing us to a tie in the birthday mini golf standings. Saying our goodbyes to Alfred, we promised to come and see him any time we were in the area. We walked slowly back to the car. As we walked, Travis' arm would brush my arm and my hand would brush his hand, creating sparks in my stomach. I tried to hold my hands in front of me to keep from touching him, but his arm would always brush against mine, causing those flutters to linger.

Travis opened my door when we got to the car and I slowly sank into the seat, as lady-like as I could in the dress. I leaned my head against the headrest and closed my eyes trying to once again calm my nerves. Travis slid into the driver's seat and started the car, honking as we exited the parking lot.

My left hand was resting on the seat next to me, and I glanced over to see Travis' semi resting on the shifter. His thumb and forefinger were on the shifter, while the other three were dangling off, dangerously close to my hand. I felt my hand twitch at the closeness of his hand and watched as his hand slowly dropped off the shifter and rested right next to mine, with our pinkies overlapping.

The butterflies returned at that simple touch.

What the crap is going on?!

Chapter Sixteen

Travis pulled into the driveway of the house. I glanced down at our hands which had become fully entwined during the hour drive. The fluttering in my stomach never slowed and I was positive I was about to throw up any moment.

This has to be a dream. A weird freaky...fantastic dream.

"So, as much as I want to hang out with you for the rest of the day, I'm due back at the guest house to meet with Jim. He really isn't doing well with there being only six girls left." He turned to me, releasing my hand. "But I will be back tonight for dinner with all of you ladies."

My smile faltered for a second. "Well, thanks for hanging out with me today. I'm glad I could steal you away for a little while."

I opened my door, stepped out of the car and closed the door before my face could give me away. I started walking back to the house, tears forming in my eyes.

Why am I crying?

"Riles," Travis called out to me, rolling down the window. I blinked back the stupid tears and turned to face his car. He was leaning across the passenger seat staring at me out the window. "This isn't over."

Before I could even digest what he meant, he winked at me and drove off down the driveway. I turned back to the house more confused than ever.

After heading into the house and being bombarded by the girls about our date, I decided to spend the rest of the day relaxing out by the pool. It was a beautiful day and I didn't want to be stuck in the house with the other girls for the rest of the day. There was a light breeze coming off the lake, making sitting outside in the summer dress very comfortable.

My mind went back to what Travis had said in the car when we got back to the house. For whatever reason, I had thought that what happened at Al's would have maybe changed things for this stupid show. I mean, we almost kissed. Travis and I almost *kissed*. I'm going to assume those fluttery feelings I had every time he touched me today was because things were shifting between us. I thought maybe Travis would want to figure this out between us. Put the other girls to the side and figure us out. I was his freaking best friend after all. We had history! Clearly there was *something* there. Shouldn't he want to be with me over the other girls? Or was I just hoping that's what he wanted?

Oh my goodness, was I the only one who felt the stupid flutters? Was *I* the one who almost kissed *him*?

Groaning, I slammed my head back against the chair. This was getting way too confusing. I had no idea what I was feeling for him anyway, and I needed to stop over analyzing everything.

Someone plopped down in the chair next to me. "Hey you."

I lifted my head up, shielding my eyes with my hand, and looked over at the culprit interrupting my thoughts. I found Taylor stretched out on the chair, with her head tilted up to the sun, drinking it in.

I smiled over at her, glad it was Taylor and not any of the other girls. Taylor was the only girl I really got along well with. I would say in the last two weeks we had become friends—well, as much of friends as we could be, with me withholding information and all. I often wondered what would happen if she found out who I really was. Would she be pissed that I've been lying to her? Would she be happy I wasn't actually competition? Would she just not really care either way? I guess I would find out when the show was over and she knew.

"Hey Taylor." I leaned my head back against my chair, soaking up the sun again.

"I'm not sure if you wanted to be alone out here, but those girls were driving me crazy!" Taylor groaned from her seat.

I started to laugh. "That's exactly why I'm out here! I just didn't want to deal with them today!"

"Nicki has been complaining all day about you being the first individual date. She thinks she deserved it over anyone else in the house." Taylor got up to grab two waters out of the outdoor fridge before returning to her seat and handing me one.

"Thanks." I took the water and gratefully took a drink. "Nicki is obnoxious. She thinks the world revolves around her. I have no idea what Travis sees in her."

"She flaunts herself around him. Have you seen how low cut her shirts are? Any guy would want to keep her around." Taylor scowled, glaring up at the house.

"But I thought Travis was different than that." Even though I knew exactly how he was, and Nicki was the type of girl he usually went for. I just thought this show would maybe have changed his mind.

"Maybe we just need to change his view on things. I see you're wearing a dress today. That's a first since we've gotten here." Taylor mentioned it as casually as she could, though the giant smirk on her face gave her away.

"Hey, it was a gift from… Um… It was a gift from a friend." I stumbled over my almost give-away. I glanced over at her, but she still had her head back against the chair with her eyes closed.

That was close.

"Well, you look amazing in it. And I know Travis noticed."

"What do you mean, noticed?" I was curious. Maybe the chemistry between Travis and I wasn't just all in my head.

"Don't hate me, but I glanced out the window when you left. I saw the way he looked at you when you walked out. And how you flew into his arms. I swear, if I wasn't a part of this competition, you two make the cutest couple." Taylor glanced over at me with a wicked grin.

"Psht, please. He didn't look at me any differently than he usually does." I brushed it off like it meant nothing, but my heart was beating faster at the thought of Travis actually seeing me as something other than his best friend.

"Sweetie, I know what I saw. And the dazzling smile he broke into when you walked out totally gave it away. He definitely has a thing for you," Taylor explained. I was in shock that she was taking this all with ease. If it had been anyone else, they would probably be clawing my eyes out.

"I think he may just act that way towards everyone." I brushed off Taylor's statement. I wasn't going to let my heart believe something like that. Especially when this is all playing out on a TV show. If Travis liked me, he would have mentioned something well before now. Wouldn't he?

"Isn't that why we are all here? To get Travis to notice us, to fall for us? Why are you trying to push this away when it's what everyone would love to have?" Taylor sat up and swung her legs to the side of the chair facing me; she placed her elbows on her knees and leaned slightly forward, getting closer to me.

Sighing I sat up and faced her, mimicking her pose. "I don't know Taylor. Maybe I just don't belong here. I'm not really good at putting my feelings out for the whole world to see."

"Then why did you sign up?" She was curious, I couldn't really blame her.

"I was kind of forced into it by my best friend and his mom." It wasn't a lie—I just wasn't about to mention who my best friend really was.

"You must have one hell of a relationship with them, for them to be able to force you into doing this." Smiling at me, she stood up and started to stretch.

"You have no idea," I mumbled standing with her.

"I suppose, we better get ready for dinner," Taylor said as she started walking towards the house, waving for me to follow.

"You know about that?" I was shocked she knew, but obviously she would have been told.

Taylor laughed. "Yes, we got a note shortly after you left on your date about having a birthday dinner."

"Why do they have to make such a big deal about my birthday? It's not like everyone here likes me…" I trailed off, seeing Nicki sneering at me from the patio door.

"Speak of the devil." Taylor leaned in and whispered to me. I started laughing, Taylor joining in as we pushed open the door and walked into the living room.

"What are you two so happy about?" Nicki glared at us. Apparently anyone being happy wasn't okay around her.

"Is it a crime to laugh Nicki?" Taylor threw back at her with a glare of her own. "Just because you want to be bitchy all the time, doesn't mean everyone else feels the same way." She turned to me, giving me a wink, then scurried up the stairs before Nicki could respond.

That little traitor left me in the hornet's nest!

I stood frozen for about a millisecond watching Taylor's retreat before I heard Nicki utter a few choice words under her breath. I glanced her way, noticed the fury in her eyes and decided to take Taylor's lead and run up to my room before she could throw angry insults my way.

Travis arrived at 5:30 and popped a bottle of champagne. "To Riley, may your 26th year be even better than the last 25!" He held up his glass and the girls followed suit, except for Nicki, who just drank her champagne down in a gulp and grabbed the bottle for a refill.

I should have been more embarrassed about the toast, but Travis was staring at me with such genuine happiness that I couldn't do anything but lift my glass and smile right along with him. He ushered us into the dining room where the food was spread out on the table. I started laughing as soon as I entered the room.

"We're having Chinese take-out?" Nicki slurred, having consumed four glasses of champagne in about fifteen minutes.

"Well, word is Riley loves Chinese take-out." Travis mentioned, leaving out the fact that we had made it a tradition to get Chinese take-out, rent a movie and veg out on the couch for both of our birthdays, years ago.

"Thank you," I whispered, settling into my seat.

Everyone was silent as we dug into the food. I loaded my plate with Hunan chicken, vegetable lo mien and an egg roll. I glanced up to see Nicki scooping a little steamed chicken and broccoli on her plate. She pushed it around and picked at it but never actually ate anything.

Travis and I usually stuffed ourselves silly with food, and then sprawled out on the couch not moving for hours. I figured I should take it easy today, so only had the one plate. There were a ton of leftovers, which Travis quickly scooped up and took to the kitchen to put away.

I offered to help Travis, but he declined to let anyone help. So I sat at the table in quiet conversation with Taylor and Kara.

Travis returned from the kitchen carrying a gourmet lemon and raspberry cake with 26 candles on it. He set it in front of me, whispering in my ear, "You didn't think I forgot, did you?"

I looked up smiling while Travis led the girls in singing happy birthday. When they finished, I blew out the candles in one breath.

Travis clapped his hands, "Well, who wants cake?" He started slicing the cake and scooping it onto plates and handing them to the waiting girls.

The cake was melt in your mouth delicious and we ate mostly in silence. Every year, since I'd discovered the genius of lemon and raspberry together, I had some sort of dessert with those flavors for my birthday. Each year, Travis tried to top what I had the year before. It went from a simple lemon cake with raspberry frosting, to delicious raspberry filled lemon cupcakes, to raspberry-lemon ice cream, to the most amazing raspberry macaron filled with lemon buttercream that Travis had flown in from effing Paris.

116 | CAYLIE MARCOE

"I'm going to take the rest of the cake into the kitchen for the crew to enjoy." Travis broke me out of my thoughts as he stood and gathered the leftover cake. He glanced over at me and winked, nodding his head slightly to the doorway and headed out to the kitchen.

"Happy Birthday, Riley! It's so exciting that you get to celebrate here!" Taylor smiled at me from across the table.

"Thanks, Taylor. It has been a pretty great day," I said, smiling back, genuinely happy I was celebrating with her.

"Yes, nothing better than getting pampered by Travis," Nicki scoffed.

I looked at Taylor and rolled my eyes in Nicki's direction. Taylor giggled and got an evil eye from Nicki before quickly turning to Kara next to her and engaging her in conversation.

"If you'll excuse me, I have to use the restroom." I pushed back from the table and headed out to the hallway.

I was halfway down the hall when a door opened to my left and I was pulled in. Immediately I was pressed against the door, with Travis' arms propped on either side of my head, and his hard body pressed against me.

"Happy Birthday Riles," he murmured, gently pressing a kiss on my forehead.

My body erupted with heat at the closeness of his. He trailed kisses down to my ear where he whispered, "Do you have to look so amazing all the time?"

I honestly didn't think I could get more confused by this whole situation, yet here I was, completely baffled as to what was going on.

"Trav, I look like I always do." My voice came out hoarse. His lips were so close to mine at this point, my brain was not functioning at all.

Honestly, all I wanted to know was what his lips felt like.

Ohmygod, he's your best friend! Stop it!

"Riles, I…" Travis' eyes were on my mouth. He flicked his tongue across his lips and leaned slightly more into me. I could smell the lemon on his breath as I watched his lips move even closer to mine.

Was this really happening?

I clenched my hands into a fist, pinching my skin with my nails. *Ouch. Yep, this was real.*

My heart thudding in my chest and if I looked down I would be able to see my shirt moving—it was beating so fast. I heard the buzz of the cameras that were positioned throughout the room as it was repositioned and probably zoomed in on us.

I held my breath and my eyes fluttered closed as Travis' lips lightly brushed against mine. He moved his left hand from the door to my cheek, lightly running his thumb over it. He pressed harder against my mouth, running his tongue across my bottom lip and a moan escaped my lips. He pulled back just enough to separate our lips, both of us with quick breaths and the smell of lemon and raspberry lingering around us.

"Was that…" I stopped and shook my head. I couldn't think clearly. My mind was racing with thoughts of the kiss and hoping it would happen again.

"Riles…" Travis cupped my face with his hands, bringing my mouth back to his.

Before our lips could meet again someone started banging loudly on the door behind me. "The ladies are starting to wonder where you two are. Better get back out there, unless you want one of them to find you." Someone from the crew yelled.

Travis stepped back from me and ran his hand through his hair. "Um… so, yeah, Happy Birthday," he said glancing around the room. "I guess I should get back out there."

I nodded and moved away from the door so he could get out. He opened the door a crack before stopping and turning back to me.

"Come over tonight. Okay?" he said, staring intently into my eyes.

I found myself nodding again, unable to form words. He gave me a small smirk before heading out into the hall and closing the door quietly behind him.

I slowly sank into the nearest chair and exhaled slowly.

Well, that was…amazing.

Chapter Seventeen

I'd been standing outside of Travis' door for the last twenty minutes, unable to actually knock. What was I thinking coming over here? Either it was going to be completely awkward on the other side of that door, or it was going to be…completely awkward.

Yep, either way—awkward.

I lifted my fist again, debating on knocking, when the door cracked open.

"Are you just going to stand out there all night? Or do you actually want to come in?" Travis grinned from behind the door.

"How long have you known I was here?" I asked, walking through the door.

"Oh, you know…when you showed up twenty minutes ago." Travis laughed and dodged my arm as I tried to smack him.

"You could have rescued me earlier!" I yelled as he took off for the living room.

I followed him past the kitchen into the living room, where we had never hung out before. It was fitted with an overstuffed couch and a large flat screen TV attached to the wall. Two chairs flanked either side of the couch with a cherry wood coffee table in the middle. The wall behind the couch had a patio door, which was cracked open allowing a light breeze to flow through the room.

Was it weird that we've always had conversations and hung out in his bedroom? And why were we now in the living room? Did he feel awkward about having me in his bedroom after the kiss?

Oh my God. Was I a horrible kisser?!

"Riles?" Travis waved his hand in front of my face, breaking me out of my thoughts.

I blinked up at him. "Uh...what?"

He laughed. "I asked which movie you wanted to watch." He was holding up two new movies: a romantic comedy and an action movie.

"Oh, um...that one." I pointed at the action movie. I was not in the mood to watch romance with this man. I walked over and sat down on the couch, pulling my feet up under me and snuggling into one of the pillows.

Travis walked over to the DVD player and put the movie in before returning back to the couch and sitting right next to me. He held up the remote to turn on the TV then hit play on the DVD remote.

I wasn't paying any attention to what was on the TV. I couldn't stop myself from glancing over at Travis every two seconds. He was in his pajamas and was sitting so close I could smell the citrus soap he used in the shower, along with the woodsy minty smell that was uniquely Travis. He had draped his arm across the back of the couch behind me, and was mindlessly running his fingers through my hair.

Each time I felt the pull of my hair in his fingers, a chill would run through my body. It got to the point where I looked like I was shivering before he noticed the effect he was having on me.

"Are you cold?" He rubbed his hand down my shoulder, making the shivers worse.

"Um...I don't...uh...know," I stuttered, unable to form a complete sentence once again today.

Ugh, I do not like this awkwardness.

He grabbed the flannel blanket draped across the back of the couch and threw it over both of us. Then threw his arm over my shoulder again, pulling me closer to him.

I laid my head against his shoulder, my body fitting perfectly against his. Shifting my head a little, I breathed him in, relaxing for the first time since the kiss. Which was strange, I would have thought the touching would be extremely awkward.

Staring at the TV I tried to take slow deep breaths to calm myself. I could feel my heart beat exceedingly fast and the butterflies in my stomach would not settle down. My fingers were starting to twitch with the overwhelming amount of nervous energy coursing through my body.

Settle down, Riley.

I took another deep breath and held it, counting to ten before slowly releasing. Nope, didn't help at all. Travis was still absentmindedly running his fingers up and down my arm, which was not helping any. I decided I couldn't take any more of these damn nerves and tried to scoot myself into a sitting position. As soon as I attempted to move, Travis locked his arm around me, making it impossible for me to budge.

"Trav, I really need to sit up." I complained into his chest. Seriously, if I couldn't get away from his delicious scent I was going to start hyperventilating.

I felt his laugh before I heard it. I smacked his stomach, angry that he was finding this all funny while I was on the verge of a panic attack.

"Riles, it was just a kiss." Travis let me sit up, but still kept his arm around me.

"Just...just a kiss?" I looked at him questioningly. Really, that's all it was to him?

"It's your birthday; it's a birthday kiss." He shrugged, glancing back at the TV.

At those words, the flutters disappeared. Right now I had the uncontrollable urge to punch him, repeatedly. Angrily I brushed off his arm and stood up and started pacing in front of the couch.

"Riles, you're in the way." Travis kept moving his head trying to watch the movie.

Really, he wants to watch the movie right now?!

"Travis, we've celebrated 15 of my birthdays together, before this one. Not one year did I ever get a damn birthday kiss from you!" I stopped right in front of the TV and glared at him. "So, tell me, why now? Why this year?"

Travis laughed and leaned his head back against the couch. "Riles, I was just trying to ease the tension. I could physically feel you freaking out on me. I wasn't sure if it was because you were uncomfortable with the kiss and didn't know how to act around me, or if it was the opposite." He reached out to grab my hand. "So, I just decided to go for one option and see how you reacted." He gave a little tug on my hand, causing me to stumble forward.

"And can I say, I'm really pleased with this reaction," he said as he tugged again, harder this time, forcing me to fall forward and straddle his lap.

Yeah... I definitely should not be sitting on Travis like this.

I tried to push off of him, but he wrapped his arms around my waist, locking them behind me. Once again, making it impossible for me to move.

"Trav, what's going on here?" I whispered unable to make eye contact with him.

"I think you have a pretty good idea." He smirked and unwrapped one hand from my waist and brought it up to my face.

Slowly, ever so slowly, he inched towards me, until his lips were mere centimeters from mine. "I've been thinking about doing this again since I left you in that room," he mumbled against my lips, before pressing his against mine.

I didn't have time to react, nor did I care to. All I knew was Travis was kissing me again, and the butterflies took full flight in my stomach. Where the first kiss was short and timid, this kiss was all power. Travis quickly ran his tongue across my bottom lip and I opened to him. Our tongues met with a moan, from me or from Travis, I'm not sure. Without breaking the kiss, Travis laid me down on the couch and hovered over me, propped up on one elbow. His other hand found the hem of my shirt and slipped under it, running his fingers lightly against my skin. I heard a moan escape from my lips as chills ran through my body from the skin-to-skin contact.

Travis moved his mouth from mine and started trailing kisses along my jaw and down my neck. I tried catching my breath, but Travis hit a spot by my ear that caused my hips to buck up and a hiss to escape from my mouth. Thousands of sparks flew through my body. I had to bite my bottom lip to keep from moaning.

I felt Travis' smile against my skin. "Found it," he mumbled and resumed kissing around the spot.

He teased me for what felt like hours, lightly rubbing his hand up and down my waist, and kissing my neck, but never that spot or my lips. I finally reached up and grabbed his head, pulling him back down to my lips. He tasted of spicy cinnamon from his toothpaste.

Shit, did I brush my teeth before coming over?

I couldn't continue to ponder my thought, because Travis moved his mouth back to the spot by my ear. All thoughts flew from my mind and all I could focus on was the tingles traveling down my body. Travis moved his hand down and was lightly tickling my side, while his mouth was continuing its assault on my neck. My hips jerked again involuntarily.

"Trav…. Stop!" I tried brushing his hand off my side to cease the tickling, but that just caused him to tickle harder. My whole body started jerking against his hand, trying to escape the tickles. Between the tickling and the neck kissing, my brain was on overdrive.

"Trav….please!" I begged barely above a whisper, breathing heavily.

He finally stopped the tickling and brought his head back over mine. A giant smile took over his face as he leaned down and lightly brushed his lips against mine. He then tucked his body behind mine, rolling us to face the TV. The movie was almost over.

"I don't know why we waited so long to do that," he murmured in my ear.

I smiled, relaxing into him. He pulled me closer to him, leaving his arm draped across my waist. I entwined my fingers with his as exhaustion took over.

"Happy Birthday, Riles," Travis whispered in my ear as I drifted off to sleep.

Chapter Eighteen

I woke up to a dark and silent house. Without moving and waking Travis, I squinted towards the cable box to see what time it was.

Three… in the morning. Ugh.

As quietly as I could, I untangled my hand from Travis' and scooted off the couch and out of his arms. He groaned and rolled onto his stomach, but continued to sleep. I debated for a moment whether to wake him and go to the bed to sleep or to leave him and just go back up to the main house. I was just about to reach out to him and wake him, when my brain kicked in and told me it was time to leave.

As much as I loved cuddling with Travis, I needed to go to my own bed. Especially now, after everything that happened. I carefully covered Travis with the flannel blanket that had made its way down to his feet. Quietly I tiptoed into the kitchen and slipped on my shoes.

Opening the door slowly, I stepped out into the cool early morning air. I checked that the door was locked behind me and quietly closed it.

I started my way up the path from the guest house to the main house. My mind was traveling at warp speed trying to make sense of what those kisses meant for our friendship now. Or heck, what they meant for this stupid show. I mean, if I were in his position, I would choose us and move on with our lives. Is there really any question about that? We've known each other forever, it just makes sense he would pick me. I realized he was under contract with the show and wasn't able to cut it short, but seriously, after this, what kind of show will it be? Or does Travis not think like me at all, and will he still continue to 'date' the other girls?

Oh God, I never thought of that.

No, he wouldn't do that. Not after what he said tonight. He clearly feels something between the two of us too, and if he were to pursue the other girls, he would know what it would do to me. I mean, I am still a girl after all!

I was lost in thought when I opened the door to the main house. I shut it quietly, but didn't realize there was a light on.

"What were you doing out there?" Nicki's high pitched voice asked from across the kitchen.

Startled, I looked up and slammed my body back against the door. "Nicki...I...I didn't see you there."

"Clearly." She snorted. "You didn't answer me. It's three a.m. Why were you outside?"

"Not that it's any of your business, but I needed some air." I lied easily, walking quickly to the staircase.

"Like I believe that? If you needed air you could have opened a window." Nicki rolled her eyes in my direction. "You were probably trying to get Travis to let you into his house."

I felt heat creep into my cheeks. "I'm not that insecure about where I stand with him, Nicki. I don't need to sneak to his house for nightly visits to keep him interested."

Nicki glared at me, before releasing a huff and turning to leave the kitchen. I watched her back until it was out of view, then slumped against the handrail in the stairwell.

That was too close.

No more zoning out for me, I thought as I climbed the stairs. I could have dealt with anyone else catching me coming in at three a.m., but not her. Not Nicki, who has it out for me and would probably try to use this against me. Once I got to my room, I threw myself onto the bed, exhaustion once again taking hold.

***

I poured myself another cup of coffee, staring mindlessly out the window when I heard a light tap at the door. I turned and nearly dropped my mug when I saw Travis grinning at me from the other side.

"What are you doing here?" I hissed, setting my coffee on the counter and stepping outside next to him. I pushed him around the corner to the side of the house, where no one would see us.

"You know if you wanted to get me alone, there are easier ways to do it." He grinned and wrapped his arms around me, pinning me against the side of the house.

"Travis!" I squealed as he started kissing up my neck. "Seriously…stop!" I tried pushing him away, but he was persistent. He trailed kisses up my jaw and gave me a small peck on the mouth before pulling back.

"Why did you leave this morning?" He frowned as he questioned me.

I sighed and slipped out of his hold. His frown deepened.

"No Travis, it's nothing like that. I just woke up around three and decided I should just head back up here." I gently touched his arm, hoping it would relax him.

"But why didn't you wake me and tell me? Do you know what it was like to wake up with you gone?" He groaned and leaned against the house.

"Sorry. You were sleeping. I didn't want to wake you." I glanced down at the ground mumbling. "And plus, it's not the first time I've left your house while you were sleeping and didn't wake you up to say bye."

"Riles, I'm pretty sure things are completely different now." He lifted my chin so I would look at him. He gave me his sexy smirk before winking at me.

Before I could stop myself, a snort escaped. Seriously, he just winked at me!

"I'm aware of that, Trav. But I just don't know…how things stand, with being on this show and all." I felt even more confused after saying it out loud.

"I'll work it out Riles. I'm sure I have to finish the show, but *we'll* figure it out." He pulled me against him in a hard hug. "We'll figure it out. It's you. It's always you," he murmured into my hair.

"If you say so." I sighed into his chest. I wasn't sure how he was certain we could figure it out, but I trusted him.

"Riley. Travis. I think you should head your separate ways now," Jim said from behind us.

Startled, I jumped out of Travis' arms and spun to face Jim.

"Jim… um… hi." I felt the blush inch onto my cheeks. "We were just… um…"

"I'm aware of what you were just doing. You two are aware there are hidden cameras all over right? Inside. Outside. In the guest house…" He trailed off, and I blushed even more.

"Oh. I knew there were cameras in the house. Guess I didn't realize they were every other place too." I meekly spit out.

"You guys, I don't have an issue with what is going on between you two. In fact, I'm sure the ratings will be amazing. Two best friends falling in love on TV—it's gold.

But you have to keep in mind, there is still a show being filmed. We have to milk it out until the end. Travis you can't just choose Riley right now and be done. You still have to go on dates with the other girls." Jim paused looking between the two of us. "I trust this isn't going to cause an issue?"

"No sir," Travis said from behind me. All I could manage was to shake my head.

"Good. Now, Riley why don't you head back inside, mingle with the girls. Travis come with me, we'll discuss upcoming dates." Jim nodded at us expectantly.

"Uh, well… see you later." I gave Travis a little wave while making my way around the house.

"You better!" He grinned at me before heading over to Jim, who immediately started talking and heading towards the guest house.

I slipped back into the kitchen and grabbed my now cold coffee that I had set on the counter. Sighing, I poured it out into the sink and got myself a refill.

Guess this was going to be more difficult than we thought.

Chapter Nineteen

I made my way into the living room just as Addison came rushing in waving an envelope up in the air.

"We have a group date!" she squealed, causing the rest of the girls to stop what they were doing and turn to her expectantly.

Just as she started to rip open the envelope, Nicki came up beside her and grabbed it out of her hands, tearing the paper out herself. Addison cringed and moved to the side a few steps away from Nicki, who was currently reading the note to herself.

"Care to fill the rest of us in?" I glared at Nicki until she looked up from the note.

"It's a group date for all of us." Nicki rolled her eyes, "We're going swimming." She dropped the note on the side table by the sofa and stormed out of the room. "Dumbest date ever."

Addison grabbed the note again and quickly read it out loud. "Ladies, grab your swimsuits and sunscreen! Get ready for some adventure as we head out to my favorite swimming hole. I hope none of you are afraid of heights! I'll be by to pick you up at noon. Travis."

"Swimming hole?" Taylor questioned looking at me.

I shrugged, "It'll be fun. It's supposed to be a scorcher today!"

"I wonder why Nicki was so upset about it. You'd figure she'd be happy to walk around in her bikini." Kara mentioned from behind me.

I turned and smiled at her, "Maybe the whole heights thing isn't sitting with her well." My grin turned bigger when I realized where we were going and what exactly those heights were.

"What do you know?" Taylor whispered to me as we made our way up the stairs behind Addison and Kara.

"I'm just putting two and two together," I whispered back, slowing my steps. "Swimming hole and heights." I drawled out slowly for her.

Taylor just gave me a confused look and shook her head. "Sorry, no idea where your brain is."

I laughed slapping her arm lightly. "Cliff jumping." I winked at her as we made it to my room.

Her eyes went wide before a smile formed on her face. "Cliff jumping? For real? I've only jumped off a tiny man-made cliff before. I've always wanted to do the real thing." She was bouncing in her shoes.

"I can't say for certain, but I have a good feeling about it." I smiled as she squealed and skipped down the hall to her room. "See you in a few!" she called over her shoulder as she entered her room.

I pushed my door open and walked slowly over to my dresser. I never had an issue wearing swimming suits around Travis before, but right now my stomach was in knots thinking about wearing one. I pulled out my simple black with white polka dots tankini and the black board shorts I always paired with it. I've had this same swimsuit since I was 21 and Travis had an event in Hawaii. Stupid me had forgotten to pack a swimsuit, so that was the first one I grabbed when I got off the plane. It was pretty worn out, a hole forming at the bottom where I would always pull it down when getting out of the pool.

Probably should get a new one soon.

I was just about to shut the drawer when I noticed a small brown paper package with a piece of twine wrapped around it sitting in the corner of the drawer. I picked it up and walked over to sit on the bed. Slowly I pulled the twine off and unfolded the package. Inside was a beautiful navy blue tankini with cream colored roped vertical stripes. I pulled it out of the paper and held it in front of me, taking in the thick halter straps and the bust that came together with a knot. A pair of navy blue board shorts fell to the floor as I held the top up. I reached down to pick the shorts up and a note fluttered to the floor. I reached down again picking the note up and reading:

Thought you may need a new suit. You'll look amazing in it! -K

I quickly reached into the drawer on the side table and pulled out my phone.

Me: You didn't send me a new swimsuit, did you?

I tapped my fingers on the table waiting for a reply.

Mom2: No. Should I have?
Me: Ugh. No. But I'm holding a new suit, with a note from...'you'.
Mom2: I don't know why Travis doesn't just sign his own name.
Me: No kidding.
Mom2: Heading to the swimming hole today?
Me: How did you know?!

Mom2: Travis keeps me updated...

Travis keeps her updated? How updated does he keep her?!

Me: Is that all you know????
Mom2: Sweetie, I'm a mom, I know everything.
Me: Haha.
Mom2: It's about time though....
Me: Yeah... okay, I gotta get changed.
Mom2: Have fun!

I shut the phone off and tossed it back in the drawer, before gathering up the swimsuits and grabbing a pair of cut-off jean shorts and a blue and white striped tank top from my dresser. I headed to the bathroom and quickly threw on the new suit and smiled when I saw myself in the mirror.

It really wasn't much different from my last suit, which I had loved. This one was a tiny bit sexier though, which caused my stomach to knot up tighter.

Why would Travis buy me this suit?!

Sighing I pulled my jean shorts and tank on over the suit, tossed my hair up into a messy bun at the top of my head and grabbed a beach towel from the linen closet before heading back to my room. I grabbed an extra pair of shorts and another tank, stuffing them along with the towel into a canvas bag. I slipped my feet into a pair of white flip-flops and tossed the bag on my shoulder before heading out of my room. I nearly ran into Nicki as I closed the door behind me.

"Watch where you're going," she snarled at me. She was wearing a white strapless summer dress that was transparent enough I could make out her skimpy hot pink bikini underneath.

"Excuse me for walking out of my room." I rolled my eyes at her before turning and heading down the hall. I was so tired of Nicki and all her crap. She thought she was queen bee around here, and I was tempted to tell her she didn't have a chance in hell with Travis. Luckily, I caught sight of the crew at the bottom of the stairs and bit my lip before I could turn around and blow my cover.

Taylor was the only one in the living room when I entered, so I quickly made my way to sit next to her.

"You'll never believe the suit Nicki is wearing!" I whispered to her.

She laughed, "I'm sure it can't be anything worse than what she usually wears out at the pool."

I laughed thinking about all the barely there suits she had worn. Most were just good for lying out on the chairs getting a tan. If she were to jump in the water with any of them on, they would probably fall right off. The current one had spaghetti thin straps which didn't look like it would hold up to anything, much less cliff jumping. But knowing Nicki, I assumed she wouldn't even attempt to do anything adventurous.

Seriously, why did Travis keep her here?

Taylor and I stopped talking as Nicki huffed into the room. She glared at us before heading to the bar to find herself something to drink. I glanced over at Taylor whose face was twitching like she was trying to hold back a laugh. That one look undid me and I burst out laughing, Taylor finally letting go shortly after.

"What's so funny?" Nicki asked from behind us. Oddly enough, it wasn't in her usual snide voice.

"Nothing," Taylor choked out before dissolving into another giggle fit.

I had tears in my eyes from laughing so hard. Honestly, I wasn't even sure what we were laughing about anymore, but it felt good to let go.

Nicki glared at us, before rolling her eyes and grabbing a wine cooler from the bar fridge.

"Starting early, Nicki?" Kara asked as she walked into the room wearing a rainbow colored summer dress over her swimsuit. She dumped her bag on the chair before walking over to where Nicki was and grabbed a bottle of water. "Anyone else want one?" she asked lifting the bottle up.

Taylor and I both nodded our heads and Kara threw bottles at each of us. Nicki stood there sipping her drink with an evil look on her face directed towards Kara.

"Seriously Nicki, you keep looking at me like that, your face is going to be stuck in that position." Kara breezed past her, back to the chair where her belongings were.

I wanted to get up and cheer for Kara. She was the only other girl, aside from me, who wasn't putting up with Nicki's crap. As much as I loved Taylor, she still just kept her mouth shut around Nicki, even though you could see how much she wanted to burst, same with Erin. And Addison always clammed up whenever Nicki even looked at her.

Addison and Erin came bounding into the room together wearing similar white tank tops and black shorts. They looked almost identical with their pink canvas bags slung over their shoulders. The only difference between them was Erin's dirty blond hair thrown up in a ponytail, while Addison rocked that pixie cut with her black hair. I guess I had been too caught up with Travis to even realize those two had become so close. Which seemed slightly off, since they were both in this competition to win Travis over. But to each their own, right? After all, I had developed a close friendship with Taylor and I was pretty positive she wasn't going to like me much after she found out who I really was and that Travis was more than likely going to pick me.

Or at least I *hoped* he was going to choose me.

Addison and Erin were grabbing bottles of water when Travis came walking into the room, wearing a white t-shirt and a pair of board shorts in a simple plaid pattern of blue and white, with a few stripes of orange mixed through. He finished it off with some simple black flip-flops. He looked casual and...freaking hot, especially when he ran his hand through his already messy hair and gave us that devilish grin of his.

"You girls ready for an adventure?" He smirked at us, nodding his head towards the door.

The girls all gave shouts of excitement before grabbing their bags and heading out the door. Nicki had drained her drink and gave a sarcastic cheer before following behind them.

I glanced up at Travis who was now staring at me, "She's not too thrilled about it," I mentioned walking over to him.

"Don't really care what she thinks. This is going

to be a blast!" His face turned into that of a kid in a candy store. This boy was so excited to do something adventurous again.

"What about your ankle?" I asked glancing down at the boot on his foot.

"Doctor says swimming is just fine, it's healing up quicker than they thought, so I'm even allowed to take the boot off!" he explained with giddiness.

"And what does your doctor say about cliff jumping?" I asked.

Travis smirked, "He may not know about that."

I rolled my eyes and lightly smacked him, "If you hurt yourself again, it's all on you buddy."

Travis laughed and led me to the door with his hand on the small of my back, causing tingles to erupt all around that spot.

"It'll be a fun day," Travis said as we got closer to the SUV where the other girls were climbing in.

"Agreed. I'm just glad we get to go swimming on this hot day—and not like… hiking or something." I eyed him, knowing how he loved all these outdoor activities.

"Swimming is so much better." Travis agreed. "Plus, I get to see you in your new swimsuit." He leaned in and whispered in my ear, leaving butterflies in my stomach.

I wanted to smack him, but he quickly hopped in the passenger seat with a wicked grin.

Shaking my head, I squeezed into the back seat between Taylor and Kara. I slid my sunglasses over my eyes and leaned my head back against the headrest, hoping the drive to the swimming hole would be quick, because Nicki had already started complaining.

Chapter Twenty

We arrived at the swimming hole in less than twenty minutes. Everyone quickly scrambled out of the car, mostly, I'm sure, to get away from Nicki who hadn't stopped complaining since we left the driveway.

"Ladies, this way," Travis called, leading us down a winding path to the sparkling blue water.

We had parked at the top of the cliff, which was really only about fifteen feet high. A small creek ran through somewhere behind where we parked, and spit out a small waterfall into the swimming hole.

The swimming area was about as large as half a football field, which trickled out into another little creek. Since the pool was spring fed, I knew it was going to be nice and cool. I had only been outside for a few minutes and I could already feel the sweat beading up on my skin. Not only was it supposed to reach 85 degrees today, but it was supposed to be humid as hell. A thunderstorm late tonight was inevitable.

"Has anyone ever gone cliff jumping before?" Travis asked as he dropped his bag on the small beach and quickly kicked off his flip-flops.

I have!

But Travis already knew that, and I wasn't going to say it out loud in front of these girls. They were already eyeing me, waiting for me to say something, since apparently I do all the adventurous things. If only they knew...

"I have." Taylor quickly spit out. We all turned to look at her and she flushed a deep red. "I mean, I've done it once when I was on vacation with my family, years ago. And it was a tiny jump."

I glanced back at Travis who had a slow grin creeping across his face. "That's awesome!" he shouted, running over to Taylor. "Want to jump with me first?"

He looked like a child at Christmas time, all bubbly excitement. My smile stopped short when he scooped her up over his shoulder and started running with her up the path to the top of the cliff.

"We'll be right back down!" he called out over Taylor's giggles.

I twisted my hands around my bag so tightly I started to lose feeling in my fingers. I plopped down on the sand and released my hands from my bag, tossing it to the side. Ugh, was I really jealous of Taylor?

Yes, yes I was.

Oh that was ridiculous. I knew how Travis felt about me, I knew what he was doing was because we are on this stupid show and are currently surrounded by five different cameras. He had to do it—and it's not like he was making out with her or anything, he was just going to jump off a cliff with her.

But why did he have to toss her over his shoulder? That seemed too…intimate.

I rolled my eyes at myself. I was overreacting. I glanced up at the cliff as they made their way to the edge. Travis leaned down to whisper something in Taylor's ear and she beamed back at him, laughing lightly. He grabbed her hand and I felt my heart ache a little. As I watched, he counted down until the two of them leapt from the cliff and were falling into the water. They hit with a splash and quickly resurfaced laughing and splashing each other.

Oh, I'd had enough, time to get in the water with them. I stood, slipped out of my flip-flops and shed my shorts and tank.

I called to Kara who was sitting close by, "Let's get in the water!"

She launched to her feet. "Thank God, it is hot as hell out here!" And with that, we both took off running into the crisp, cool sparkling water.

We stayed in the shallow end of the water, to keep the water under the cliff clear for anyone who wanted to jump. The water where we were was up to our chests and felt amazing.

"That was exhilarating!" Taylor squealed as she swam up to us.

"It looked like fun; I really want to try it now! Though, it may be more fun with Travis," Kara mentioned glancing around the swimming hole.

"Where did he go?" Taylor asked glancing out to the beach to see if Travis had made his way over there.

I felt something brush against my ankle, then my knee and my thigh before finally settling on my waist. "Oh shit!" I exclaimed as the hands around my waist quickly pulled me under the water. I opened my eyes, blinking to adjust them and saw Travis grin at me before surfacing. I quickly made my way to the surface and took a deep breath. Travis and the girls were laughing and I quickly splashed all of them.

"Not funny!" I splashed at them again, causing them to laugh harder. I tried to give them my best glare, but knew I was going to start laughing too, so instead I turned and started heading out of the water.

"Oh, come back, I was just having fun!" Travis called out to me.

I turned and smirked, "Well, I want to have a little fun too, and jump." I turned back around and started making my way up the path.

I heard the sound of feet running up behind me, before I was scooped into Travis' arms. We went around one of the bends in the path, blocking us from the other girls.

"You want to jump with me?" Travis breathed, nuzzling his nose against my neck.

Oh boy, can't think here.

I pushed him back, "I suppose you'll do."

He grinned and planted a quick, chaste kiss on my lips before grabbing my hand and pulling me up the path.

"I knew that swimsuit would look great on you." Travis' eyes slowly dragged from my legs up to my chest.

I crossed my arms, forcing him to look up at my face. "I don't know why you just don't say the clothes are from you."

Travis just shrugged and gave me his sexy smirk.

"Does your ankle hurt at all?" I was worried about the jumping, I didn't want it to set him back any farther than he already was.

"No, not at all, it actually feels good to be out of that damn boot."

"Well, if it does start to hurt, make sure you put that boot back on and no more jumping."

"Don't worry, *Mom*, I will," Travis said as he rolled his eyes at me.

"Um, I hope you don't kiss your Mom the way you kissed me." I laughed when Travis stopped and let the words sink in.

"That's so…..ehhhh." Travis shuddered at the thought.

"Good, don't call me that again. I'm just worried about you, that's all."

"I know Riles, and that's why I love you." He pulled on my hand as I stumbled over my feet.

Loved me? We've said "I love you" to each other many times, but this time it felt different somehow.

We had made it to the edge of the cliff. I looked down and saw Kara and Taylor where I had left them. They smiled and waved up at me.

"Go Riley!" Taylor screamed up at me.

I smiled down at her and gave them a small wave back. I noticed Addison and Erin had ventured out into the water, but Nicki was currently sprawled out on her beach towel, soaking up the sun.

"She doesn't look like she's enjoying this date," I whispered up to Travis, nodding my head in Nicki's direction.

He glanced her way. "She doesn't seem to care for adventure."

"And she's the girl for you?" I asked, wondering why he still kept her here.

"Riles, I think you know the answer to that." He rolled his eyes at me again, squeezing my hand.

"You ready?" I asked. I was so ready to get back into the water. Just in the short time we were out of the water, the sweat had already started to bead up again.

Travis nodded, "On three. Ready. One, two, three!"

We jumped out and away from the cliff and started to free fall towards the water. Travis squeezed my hand, not letting it go, until we splashed into the water.

I quickly kicked my way to the surface, popping my head into the air a second before Travis. He grinned at me and quickly circled his arms around me, giving me a quick squeeze and a light kiss on the cheek.

"God I love this!" he breathed out, looking totally relaxed.

"It was the perfect day to do this. I couldn't imagine going mini golfing in this heat." I winked at him remembering our date yesterday.

Holy shit, was that really just yesterday?

It felt like ages ago. So much had happened since then.

Travis smiled lazily at me, so I splashed him lightly and quickly took off swimming towards Kara and Taylor.

We spent the next few hours swimming, jumping and splashing around. We finally called it quits when we started hearing thunder off in the distance. Well, Jim came and called us out of the water saying it was time to head home. He also mentioned there would be an elimination tonight, which none of us, including Travis, knew about.

***

I smoothed my hands down the side of my shirt. I had opted for a dressier floral sleeveless shirt for tonight's elimination show. I paired it with my favorite jeans that hugged my curves just right.

I was seriously hoping Nicki would go home tonight. She hadn't participated in the group date, at all. She didn't even get in the water, saying something about how non-chlorinated water messes with her skin. I honestly would never understand that woman. I don't know how the producers could keep her on the show much longer. I mean, she doesn't even do anything! She whines and complains about most dates, and she is the polar opposite of Travis. How is this going to boost ratings?

I don't know, maybe I just missed my quiet, uncomplicated, bitch-free life.

A crack of thunder from the storm raging outside made me jump and brought me out of my thoughts. I glanced at the clock and realized I needed to be downstairs in five minutes.

One more look in the mirror and I was out my door. I met up with Taylor in the hallway.

"Hey, that's a nasty storm out there." She winced as lightning flashed through the hallway window.

"I'm sure it'll be over soon." I shrugged and patted her lightly on the shoulder. "But if it gets worse, I'm sure the basement here is just as amazing as the rest of the house." I smiled lightly letting her know I was joking, but her face was ashen white.

"Oh, please don't say that!" she squeaked out.

"Afraid of storms." It wasn't a question. By her body language, it was a fact.

She nodded and jumped at the crack of thunder.

I put my arm around her shoulders. "You'll be fine." I reassured her, leading her down to the living room.

The night sky was brilliant through the wall of windows, which I'm sure terrified poor Taylor even more. Lightning danced across the sky every few seconds. Rain was pelting down from the sky at such a quick and rapid pace, you could already see it starting to flood a little in the low places of the backyard.

It seemed like it would be a quick and fierce storm, dropping tons of rain on us, but passing by within the hour. Which I kind of hoped would happen for Taylor's sake, considering she was visibly shaking in her spot.

Travis and Tessa quickly made their way into the room and stood before us, commanding our attention.

"Okay ladies, we're going to make this quick tonight. The storm outside is currently mild but is supposed to get worse, so we want to be able to assure that the eliminated girl is safe at the hotel before it takes a turn," Tessa said this cheerfully, like she was telling us there was a huge sale at Target.

Taylor shuddered and groaned slightly at the news. I reached out and grabbed her hand, hoping maybe it would calm her. She relaxed slightly and gave me a small smile.

"First bracelet please, Travis." Tessa ushered Travis to the box holding the bracelets, which were charcoal gray this time.

"This bracelet is going to the girl…" Travis started but was interrupted by Tessa.

"I'm sorry Travis, but no explanations tonight, we need to make this quick. Just say the girl's names, please."

Travis glanced over to Jim, who nodded and glanced outside.

"Oh, okay," Travis mumbled, "Um, Taylor."

I gave Taylor's hand a squeeze before releasing her so she could get the bracelet. Travis put it on her and gave her a hug before she returned back to her spot. She seemed slightly more relaxed than earlier, but maybe that was because she wasn't the girl who had to go out into the storm tonight and as soon the elimination finished she was probably going to make her way to the basement.

Travis held up another bracelet, "Riley."

I walked down to him and he slipped the bracelet on next to my other ones, before pulling me into a hug. "If the weather keeps up like this, can I bunk with you?" he whispered.

I laughed loudly pushing him back and shaking my head. He grinned at me and shrugged his shoulders.

Turning, I walked back to my spot, past a glaring Nicki, I couldn't help but smirk at her as I walked by.

"What was that about?" Taylor whispered when I got back to my spot.

"Oh, nothing. Just a stupid joke." I shrugged it off, turning my attention back to Travis.

"Addison." Travis held up another bracelet and slid it on Addison's wrist when she bounced her way up to him. After a quick hug she ran back to her spot all smiles. Travis picked up another bracelet. "Kara." Kara smiled and made her way to Travis who repeated the process.

Finally it was down to two, Nicki and Erin, who were called up by Tessa to stand in front of Travis.

Oh please oh please let it be Nicki who leaves.

I reached over and gripped Taylor's hand, needing her support. She glanced over at me and gave me a big smile. I was obviously not the only one who wanted Nicki to leave.

"And the final bracelet goes to?" Tessa broke the silence.

Travis twisted the bracelet in his hands looking between the two girls. His eyes quickly glanced over to Jim. I whipped my head over to see Jim give a slight nod. I turned back to Travis as he held up the bracelet.

"Nicki." Travis held the bracelet out to her, and got a scream in response. Everyone in the room jumped as Nicki jumped on Travis, wrapping her legs around him while giving him a hug.

Travis gave her a quick hug and pushed her gently off of him, then turned to Erin to say his goodbye while walking her to the door.

"Well that blows," Kara said coming up to us.

"I don't even know what is going on anymore," I muttered to them. "Apparently we can all be a total drag on the group dates and we'll still be here in the morning. Ridiculous."

I needed a drink. I couldn't handle this stupid situation anymore. I turned and stalked over to the bar, Kara and Taylor on my trail. I grabbed a hard cider from the fridge, holding it out to the two of them, who nodded their heads quickly. I grabbed two more, handing them to the girls, before popping the top off mine and taking a huge drink.

Travis came back into the room and walked over to the bar where we were still standing.

"Can I have one of those?" he asked nodding to my drink.

I grabbed another one from the fridge and slid it to him.

"Tough night?" I asked taking a sip of my drink.

"Yeah. It felt too rushed. I wish I could have at least talked and explained why I was choosing you girls." Travis took a drink of his hard cider, staring out into the backyard. "But this storm is supposed to get pretty bad, so I guess it's good that Erin is well on her way to the hotel by now."

"Ugh, I hate storms!" Taylor exclaimed, chugging her drink. She nodded her head at me and I quickly grabbed her another.

"It'll be fine," Travis said placing his arm around her shoulder and pulling her into him.

I clenched my hands around my bottle, eyeing the two of them standing there. They looked cute together and she looked completely relaxed in his arms.

Damnit, get your hands off of her Travis!

I could feel the jealousy rage through my body and was tempted to jump over the bar and claim what was mine. Or...what I thought was mine.

Just as I turned to talk to Kara to take my eyes and mind off the two of them cuddling, a flash of lightning filled the sky outside, followed quickly by an ear-splitting crack of thunder—and then the room went pitch black.

Chapter Twenty One

Taylor screamed, followed by a few other gasps.

"Okay ladies, everything is okay. We'll get the weather radio out and see what this storm is doing. Someone from the crew is going to be coming around in a minute handing out flashlights. Once you get your flashlight, if you could make your way to the basement, we want to take every safety precaution we can," Jim called out to us from the other side of the room.

"Taylor, it'll be okay, calm down," Travis said gently. I could only see them whenever the lightning flashed outside. But could tell Travis still had his arm around her and Taylor was now shaking uncontrollably.

"Come on Taylor, let's get to the basement." I walked around the bar and took her out of Travis' arm, glaring up at him, even though he couldn't see me.

"But we have to wait for the flashlights," Taylor muttered.

"Don't worry, we'll grab one on the way." I held on to her as I lead her through the living room, careful to not bump into any of the furniture. We had made it to the doorway when a crew member came up from the hallway with a flashlight in hand and carrying a box under his arm.

"Here you go ladies." He handed both of us a flashlight. I quickly turned mine on.

"Come, let's get downstairs." I tugged on Taylor, who was limply holding the flashlight in her hand.

"I just hate storms so much." She sniffled.

"I know. Once we get in the basement you'll feel better, promise." I found the basement door open with a crew member at the top.

"There are some lanterns around the rooms down there. Also there are coolers filled with drinks and some snacks. Blankets and pillows are in the closets. You'll be safe down there," he added, noticing Taylor's grip on me.

I gave him a smile and then led Taylor down the lantern lined stairs.

"They thought of everything, huh?" Taylor whispered as we made our way into the huge living area. There were a few sofas scattered around the room, with battery operated lanterns on every table, lighting the place in a soft glow. The basement must have been semi-sound proof, as I could barely make out the thunder that was non-stop upstairs. There was a stocked bar in the corner, opposite the stairs, with coolers sitting on top. On the far wall there was a huge TV, which was quite useless at the moment.

"Well, what kind of TV show would it be if they didn't keep us safe?" I asked as Taylor took a seat on one of the couches. I sat on the opposite end of the couch and folded my legs under me. I grabbed the blanket that was thrown over the arm of the couch and draped it over my legs.

"I like it down here. You can't hear or see anything that is happening up there." Taylor tilted her chin in the direction of the stairs.

The other girls and Travis started filing downstairs, followed closely by the crew, who had lost their big cameras in exchange for basic handheld video recorders.

"Great, this is turning into a home video TV show. Don't film me," Nicki complained, taking a seat in the far corner.

Rolling my eyes, I scooted over as Travis sat between Taylor and me on the couch. I couldn't help but smile when I noticed he was much closer to me than Taylor. He casually slid his hand under the blanket on my lap, resting his hand on my leg. A slight blush crept onto my cheeks and I was thankful the lighting was pretty dim.

"So, what should we do while we wait this out?" Travis asked the girls, looking at each of them. Addison and Kara had claimed the couch next to us, but Nicki was still off in the corner pouting.

"Truth or dare!" Addison exclaimed, clapping her hands.

"Oh God." I groaned under my breath. The last thing I wanted to do with this group of girls was play truth or dare. It was such an impulse game I wasn't sure I could quickly make up a lie to whatever truth they wanted. Travis squeezed my leg.

"Just don't use my name." He breathed so quietly I wasn't even sure he was talking to anyone.

I wanted to laugh that he knew what I was thinking, but I suppose he was thinking the same thing. If any of the girls were to ask him about his past, I would be in the story 95% of the time from the age eleven onward.

"I'm in." Kara grinned looking excited.

"Me too!" Taylor smiled from the other side of Travis. She was looking a lot more relaxed since we came to the basement.

"Why not?" Travis laughed, relaxing back into the couch, rubbing my leg gently.

"I feel like we're in high school, but fine." Nicki stood up and made her way to the empty couch in our circle.

All eyes turned to me, waiting expectantly.

I rolled my eyes. "Fine, I'll do it."

"We should set some rules though." Travis spoke up quickly. All eyes shot to him as he continued, "First, no dares to kiss me. I know that's what a lot of dares are all about, but right now I just don't feel comfortable doing it in front of all of you."

A few of the girls' faces fell, especially Nicki's. I had to suppress my smile. I was so glad he made that rule—I wouldn't have to see him kiss another girl, and by default have to punch her in the face.

"Also, there should be a penalty if you don't want to answer the truth or do the dare." Travis eyed the bar happily.

I followed his gaze. "Oh no." I groaned knowing where this was going.

Travis got up and walked around the bar to grab a bottle of tequila. "Shots are the penalty." He grabbed six shot glasses, a few limes from the basket on the corner of the bar, a salt shaker and a knife and cutting board, before coming back to our little circle and dropping them on the coffee table.

"I'm not sure tequila shots are a good idea," I said, staring wide-eyed at Travis.

"It'll make you all more truthful." He grinned wickedly before settling back in next to me.

The camera crew started securing spots around the circle, getting good angles of all of us.

Oh, this is not going to be good.

Travis sat forward and quickly sliced the limes into wedges and poured tequila into each shot glass before handing them out to us. He licked the back of his hand near his thumb and poured a little salt on it, passing the salt and the limes around the group. He nodded for us to do the same. After we all had a lime wedge and salty hands he lifted his shot glass.

"Here's to an interesting game of truth or dare." Travis clanked his glass to ours before licking the salt, downing the shot and sucking on the lime.

Oh hell!

I followed suit, salt-tequila-lime. I sucked every last drop of juice out of the lime in attempts to get the tequila taste out of my mouth.

The rest of the girls followed. Taylor cringed slightly when she did the shot. Addison and Kara seemed like pros—downing their shots without any facial expressions, with Kara forgoing the lime all together. Nicki sipped her tequila, taking a full five minutes to get the whole shot glass down, and she puckered her mouth when she sucked the lime.

"Okay, who wants to start?" Travis smiled to each of the girls.

"I'll go." Nicki chimed up. "Travis, truth or dare?"

"Truth."

Nicki's face fell, "Okay, have you ever had a one night stand?"

I chuckled under my breath; Travis has had his fair share of one night stands. Wonder if he was going to be truthful to the rest of the girls. Who knows what kind of light that would paint him in?

Travis chewed the inside of his cheek—it was a nervous habit of his. I'm sure he was debating on whether or not he wanted to air his dirty laundry to the girls. I really didn't see what the issue was. If the girls read anything about him, they would know the rumors. Plus, if what he says is true, he is going to choose me in the end, and I know every freaking thing about the man.

After a breath, Travis answered, "Yes I have." He glanced over at me. "I'm not proud of it."

I looked over at the other girls, judging their reaction. For the most part they all looked as if they knew this information already. Nicki now had a gleam in her eye, probably hoping he'd hook up with her later tonight.

Psht. Never going to happen, bitch.

"Okay, um, Kara, truth or dare?" Travis broke the silence, moving the game forward.

"Oh, uh… truth," Kara responded with surprise.

"Have you ever gone skinny dipping?"

Without batting an eye, Kara responded, "Of course. Many times. I'm willing to do it again if you have it in mind."

The room laughed and Travis' cheeks turned slightly pink before he cleared his throat and took a shot of tequila.

"Riley, truth or dare?" Kara asked with a laugh.

"Truth." I groaned inwardly hoping it was going to be easy.

"First kiss—what age, how and who?" she rattled off.

I paused before answering, smiling a little as I remembered exactly when and how it happened. And of course, who it was with.

"I was 11; I was over at my best friend's house for his birthday party. We were in the basement with a group of friends playing games when someone had the bright idea to play spin the bottle. Anyway, he went first, spun the bottle and it landed on me. It was the quickest most awkward peck ever!"

"Awe, your best friend was a guy? Do you still talk to him?" Taylor asked from the other side of Travis.

"Um, yeah. We're still best friends." I was glad it was dark, so the girls couldn't see the blush creeping up my face.

"How sweet would that have been if you fell in love with your best friend?" Taylor sighed.

"Yeah, stupid guy for letting you go," Travis mumbled.

I just rolled my eyes. This was all getting a little too awkward.

"Okay, um…" I eyed the girls in the group. "Nicki, truth or dare."

"Dare." Nicki didn't even hesitate in answering.

"Okay, um, I dare you to tell the truth. Have you ever cheated on a boyfriend?"

Nicki rolled her eyes, "First of all, that isn't even a dare. But since I'm sure it's all your tiny brain could even think of, I'll answer."

"Did you really just say that?" I started to push the blanket off of me. But Travis grabbed my leg before I could get up and pummel her.

Lucky her.

"Of course I have. Who hasn't?" Nicki continued without even acknowledging me. She glanced around the room, taking in everyone's slightly stunned faces. "I mean seriously, show of hands, who hasn't cheated on their partner?"

I raised my hand, along with the rest of the girls and Travis.

"Oh, well shit," Nicki mumbled and slumped back into her chair.

I really hope this changes things in Travis' eyes.

"Well this is awkward." Addison broke the silence.

"Okay Addison, which do you pick?" Nicki hissed at her.

"Oh hell, dare, why not?" She leaned forward staring at Nicki. "Give me your worst."

"I dare you to do a body shot off of Travis." Nicki smirked.

Addison glanced over at Travis warily.

Travis shrugged. "Either way you'll have to take a shot."

"Oh what the hell, lift your shirt up, I'm going to lick some salt off those abs." Addison grinned, pouring herself a shot. Nicki's face turned sour as Addison accepted her dare; apparently she thought Addison was going to be too shy to do anything like that. I kind of loved that Addison proved her wrong—and kind of hated Addison for what she was about to do.

Travis laughed and grabbed a lime wedge, he lifted his shirt, and he rubbed the lime lightly across a small portion of his stomach. He then placed the lime between his teeth. Addison knelt in front of him, shaking salt lightly on the wet spot left by the lime.

"You ready?" She didn't wait for a response as she ducked her head and dragged her tongue across Travis' stomach, licking up the salt. For good measure, or just to piss me off even more, she ran her tongue back over the space, then placed small kisses over the spot.

Travis knew me better than I thought, as he gripped my leg to keep me in place. Seriously, were these girls asking to get punched tonight?

We all watched as Addison slowly ran her body up against his until her mouth was right next to his. She gave him a smirk, downed the shot and immediately latched onto his mouth, sucking the juice from the lime and sneaking in a kiss along with it.

When she pulled back, she had the lime between her smug lips. I balled my fists in my lap and bit my lip to keep from jumping at her.

Seriously, when did I become this hostile? It must be the alcohol.

"You broke the rules, Addison." Travis rubbed his thumb across his lips grinning. "I think that calls for another shot."

"Well worth it." Addison laughed, pouring herself another shot and shooting it. She settled back into her seat before speaking up again. "Taylor, you've been way too quiet over there, truth or dare?"

"I thought if I just kept quiet, you all would forget about me." Taylor spoke up from the other side of Travis.

"No way, if I have to play, so do you!" I leaned in front of Travis giving her a wink.

She just rolled her eyes in my direction and answered Addison with, "Truth."

"What is your wildest sexual fantasy?" Addison slurred out. Apparently the few shots she had were quickly catching up to her.

"What?!" Taylor exclaimed. "No, no, I can't answer that!"

"Guess you'll be doing a shot then." Nicki grabbed the tequila and poured Taylor a shot.

"Oh come on! That was hardly a fair question!" Taylor exclaimed begrudgingly taking the shot Nicki was holding out. She frowned at the shot glass, but downed it like a pro.

"Okay, Travis, truth or dare?" Taylor asked as she set the shot glass back on the coffee table.

"Probably should do a dare this time," he said sounding both excited and nervous.

"Ha, okay, I dare you to do a quick strip tease…say 60 seconds." The room burst out laughing.

"Oh, you have to do this!" Kara exclaimed.

"Yes, definitely, we need to see those abs again!" Addison added.

Nicki looked like she was about to attack him.

"Oh fine. I pick the music though, and someone needs to be on the timer." Travis stood and pulled out his phone, scrolling through his music list.

"I'll be the timer!" I all but yelled. At least I could have control over something in this situation.

"Why do you get to keep your phone?" Nicki whined.

"Because I'm awesome." Travis smirked. "But really, I have some important calls to take throughout the day; I need to have my phone." He pulled up a song and handed me his phone. "Just hit play when I'm ready, then up here is the timer, start it when I start."

I glanced down at the phone and burst out laughing. He had "Pour Some Sugar on Me" selected to play. Before anyone could question my outburst Travis had moved to the open area at the end of the couch and cleared his throat, nodding at me to start the music.

I pushed play then quickly started the timer. No way was I letting this go longer than a minute.

Travis started moving his hips side to side with the music. As great of an athlete as he was, he was a horrible dancer. He started unbuttoning his plaid shirt slowly. Finally he reached the last button and let the shirt fall from his shoulder then twirled it over his head before flinging it across the room. A few of the girls screamed with excitement. I just glanced at the timer hoping it showed the minute was up.

Nope. Only twenty seconds have gone by. What the crap? What else is he going to take off?

Travis started thrusting his hips and reached down to unbutton his pants.

More screaming from the horny beasts in the room.

I looked down again, 30 seconds left. When I glanced back up at Travis, he had his pants unbuttoned and was slowly unzipping them.

Nope. Not happening!

"Time! Time's up!" I screamed into the room. I flicked off the music, plunging us into silence. At the same moment, the electricity came back up, lighting up the room, nearly blinding us all.

Travis gave us all his sexy smirk, zipped and buttoned his pants before walking over to grab his shirt. Once he had that back on, he walked over to me and took his phone back.

"Ladies and Travis, the storm has officially passed us and it is clear to head back upstairs now." Jim announced from the bottom of the steps.

"Well, I guess that concludes our truth or dare night." Travis laughed at the groans from the girls.

"But it was just getting good!" Addison complained as she stood up and followed Kara and Nicki to the stairs.

Taylor stood up next and turned to us. "Thank you for looking out for me tonight. I know I was being a big baby about it all."

"I was glad to help." I smiled at her.

Taylor paused at the bottom step looking at me. "Are you going to come up?"

"Oh, um, I'm going to help Travis clean up," I said.

"Okay. See you tomorrow." She waved at us as she headed upstairs.

"Good night," Travis called up to her as she walked out of sight.

I grabbed the shot glasses and tequila from the table and took them over to the bar sink. I placed the tequila back on the shelf and started washing the glasses, while Travis came up behind me with the cutting board and knife.

"I saw what you did there," he whispered in my ear, sending chills through my body.

"Yeah, what was that?" I asked, even though I knew exactly what he was talking about. I finished rinsing the last glass when Travis spun me around, placing his hands on the sink on either side of me.

"You stopped at forty seconds. I still had twenty more seconds to show the ladies what I got!" he whispered it in my ear before placing kisses along my jawline.

"Yeah. The *ladies* don't need to see what you have." I breathed, leaning into his kisses. "And I felt bad for you, so I called it early." It was a lie. And now Travis knew just how much I liked him.

Travis laughed against my neck. "You got it bad."

"Shut up!" I shoved him slightly smiling.

"Come here." He pulled me into his arms, placing a soft kiss on my lips, before pulling me into a hug.

"Suppose we should go upstairs," I mumbled into his chest, not wanting to let him go.

"Suppose so." He sighed pulling away from me. "If it stops raining, come over tonight." He walked me to the stairs.

"We'll see." I winked at him, before bolting up the stairs, hearing his laughter behind me.

I made it to my room without bumping into anyone else. Exhausted from either the time or the alcohol, I collapsed on the bed, pulling the quilt over me and falling quickly asleep.

Chapter Twenty Two

A few days passed and Travis and I fell into a routine. He'd come to the house and visit with the girls. He was as big a flirt as ever to the ladies, which definitely tested my patience. He had a one-on-one date with Addison, and that night at elimination he sent her home. He told me afterward that she talked about her ex the entire time and it was very clear she wasn't over him. In fact, Addison looked relieved to be leaving.

So now it was down to four—Kara, Nicki, Taylor and I. Two more eliminations until the finale and then the show was over. I couldn't wait.

This morning a note arrived for Taylor announcing she had the individual date with Travis today. She had been a nervous wreck all morning long, not knowing what to wear or how to do her hair or what to talk about. Finally I took pity on her and picked out an outfit, styled her hair in a soft side braid and gave her a pep talk. She seemed a lot calmer when Travis came to pick her up at six for their dinner date.

I was sitting in a chair by the fire when Taylor came through the front door and made a beeline towards me. She plopped down in the chair next to me with a huge grin on her face. She had literally just gotten back from her date with Travis, and she looked ready to spill everything.

"So…" I started, giving her a chance to settle into the chair and kick off her shoes.

"Oh my goodness Riley, he is *so* amazing!" she gushed, turning to face me.

I tried to keep a smile plastered on my face, but seeing her blushed cheeks and her obvious excitement caused my grin to fall a little.

"Care to spill the details?" I leaned into her, pretending like I really wanted to know, when really my heart felt like it might explode at any moment.

"It was just a simple date, a stroll around downtown and dinner afterward. But I loved it. We were able to talk, and I got to know Travis so much better. The same with him, I felt like he didn't even know I existed, and now..." She trailed off with stars in her eyes.

"Well I'm glad you two know each other now." I offered, trying to keep the small smile in place.

She leaned closer to me. "He held my hand," she whispered.

Held her hand? What are we twelve?

"That's awesome." I tried to say it with feeling, but I'm pretty sure it came out flat.

"It was romantic. He held my hand as we walked around and throughout dinner he would reach over and touch my hand." Taylor had a dreamy look in her eyes, and I kind of wanted to roll mine.

I know I should be happy for her. And I would be—if she were talking about any other guy than Travis. But the fact that it was indeed with Travis, made me want to throw up. All I could do was give a slight smile and nod.

"The best part though..." Taylor sighed, "When we got back here, he walked me to the door." She lightly touched her lips and I wanted to jump out of my seat and claw her eyes out.

Don't say it, don't say it!

"He gave me the sweetest goodnight kiss," she whispered to me with a dazzling smile on her face.

I felt like someone had punched me in the gut. I held the smile on my face though.

"That's…great." I managed to get out.

"Oh shoot. I'm sorry Riley, I shouldn't have said all of that. I forgot for a moment we are both here for Travis," Taylor apologized quickly.

"No, no, that's okay. You're excited. I'd be dying to tell someone too." I tried to play it off like it was cool. Taylor nodded and smiled at me before diving into more details about their date.

I didn't hear a word she said after that. I was trying to calm the jealousy I could feel coursing throughout my body. I knew if I didn't keep that in check, I would have to punch the poor girl. She didn't deserve it; after all she doesn't know who I am, or how Travis and I feel about each other.

Or maybe it's how I feel about Travis. Because one would think if he felt the same way, he wouldn't be kissing other girls, even if it was just a quick peck.

Taylor had paused in her conversation, so I took that opportunity to yawn loudly.

"Oh, sorry." I covered my mouth with my hand. "I guess I'm more tired than I thought. I think I'm going to head up to bed." I stood up and grabbed the book I was reading before Taylor came home.

She smiled up at me, "Have a good night."

"Night," I whispered. I quickly made my way to the staircase and ran up to my room.

Once inside the safety of my room, I fell down on the bed, grabbing my phone out of the side table.

Me: Why?

I tossed the phone on the bed next to me while I leaned back into the pillows. I was about to grab my book to start reading again, when my phone buzzed.

Trav: Riles, it's not what you think.
Me: I think Taylor explained it pretty well.
Trav: Then you would know it was just a dinner date. Nothing more.
Me: Ha. Just dinner? What about holding hands?
Trav: What are we 12?!

I laughed that his comment was exactly what I had thought.

Trav: I still have to pretend I like these girls.
Me: DO you like these girls?

I didn't really want to know the answer to that, but I had to ask. It felt like forever before my phone buzzed again.

Trav: Not like I like you...
Me: What does that mean?!?
Trav: I don't know Riles.
Me: You kissed her Trav.

No response. I threw the phone on the bed as I got up and grabbed my pajamas and headed to the bathroom. After I was changed into my plaid pajama shorts and a baggy charcoal t-shirt and my face was washed, I headed back into the room. I switched the light off as I walked past and crawled into bed. Turning on the lamp on my bedside table, I pulled the blankets over myself. Just as I got comfortable and opened the book I was reading, my phone buzzed.

Trav: It wasn't anything.
Me: Great. I'll go find Milo and start making out with him.
Trav: That is completely different!
Me: I don't see how.

I knew I was getting on his nerves by bringing Milo up. He never really cared for the guy I casually saw whenever we were in the state. I never understood why though, since Travis always had a different girl all the time. I at least stuck with one guy.

Trav: Yeah, because you actually have feelings for him.
Me: Had feelings, Trav. And you can't say you don't have any for Taylor.
Trav: Fine! I may have feelings for the girls here. But it doesn't mean anything!
Me: You kissed her.
Trav: Riles! It was just a goodnight kiss!
Me: There is really no such thing.
Trav: Stop being so jealous.
Me: I'll stop being jealous when you stop kissing other girls!
Trav: I HAVE TO DO IT FOR THE SHOW!!
Me: Fine! Whatever. You can kiss the other girls whenever you want.
Trav: ...but??
Me: Kiss the other girls, forget about kissing me.

I tossed the phone on the pillow next to me, not caring for a response from him. I probably was being overly jealous, but I honestly couldn't help it. When Taylor said they had kissed, all I saw was red. By no means did I think we were dating, but I would have hoped our fifteen years of friendship would have solidified something between us. Maybe I really was the only one feeling something between us. My phone buzzed next to me and I hesitated to even check it. I waited for a few moments before reaching over and grabbing the phone.

Trav: But I like kissing you.

I cracked a tiny smile but didn't respond back. Instead I put the phone back in the drawer, settled back into my pillows, and opened my book, hoping to take my mind off of this stupid show.

Chapter Twenty Three

Trav: Where are you??

I laughed and jogged up the path to the guest house from the beach. I walked in the back door without knocking and found Travis pacing the kitchen staring at his phone, oblivious to the fact that I was standing behind him.

"I'm here."

Travis jumped, dropped his phone and spun around. "Damn woman, you're sneaky."

I laughed and scooped up his phone from the floor. "I suppose we should get going, don't want to be late getting the boot off for good."

"Yes! Finally!" Travis exclaimed, grabbing his keys and pulling me out the side door into the garage.

We settled into the car and Travis took off down the driveway.

Since his individual date with Taylor, I had kept a slight distance from Travis. I wanted him to decide for himself what he really wanted. He did hear me when I said I wasn't going to kiss him if he was kissing the other girls. In the past week, no other girls had flaunted that he'd kissed them. Still I'd kept our kisses to small pecks when I would arrive and leave his place at night.

As I was leaving last night he mentioned he had a doctor's appointment the next day to remove his boot once and for all and he wanted me to go with. Of course I couldn't turn that down, especially since I usually accompanied him to his doctor appointments anyway as his personal assistant. And I got to spend some time alone with Travis, undocumented. The tricky part was trying to get out of the house this morning without the girls wondering where I was for two plus hours. Luckily, I had taken up those morning runs and no one questioned me as I left the house this morning.

"Um, aren't we going in the wrong direction?" I asked once I noticed we were heading in the opposite direction from the city.

"I wanted some alone time with you." He smiled over at me before turning his attention back to the road.

"But what about your boot?" I knew he had been anxious to get it off, I couldn't see him just making the whole doctor's appointment up.

"Promise you won't be mad?"

"Why would I be mad? I get to spend time with you completely uninterrupted." In fact now I was getting more excited that it was just going to be Travis and me for the next few hours.

"I got it off yesterday. I told Jim I had a meeting with my agent and I actually went to the doctor. Jim knew I didn't want cameras following me around to my personal appointments, so I may have lied a little as to what day the doctor's appointment was on. And I had to tell you what I told Jim, so if you and he ever talked about it, the stories would align," Travis explained as if he had been plotting it for days.

"So you planned all of this just to hang out with me?"

Travis laughed. "Yes, to hang out with you and talk to you about everything that is going on with this show. I feel like I should be completely honest with you, and I really don't want to discuss these things on camera."

Be completely honest with me? This cannot be good.

"Are you going to make me cry?" I couldn't help but ask.

"What?" Travis whipped his head to look at me, swerving the car slightly. He quickly focused back on the road adjusting the car, but kept sneaking quick glances at me. "Why would you ask that?"

"You said you were going to be completely honest. That makes me think the worst." I shrugged. Was I the only one listening to this conversation?

"What about the boot?" I asked pointing to what was currently covering his foot.

"Decoy. I'm taking it off, once and for all, when we get to our destination." Travis grinned.

He turned down a dirt road and we continued the ride in bumpy silence. I glanced out the window staring mindlessly at the trees passing by, thinking over every bad scenario I could possibly come up with. I turned my head, about to question Travis, but stopped when I saw the cottage in the distance.

"We're going to your parent's cottage?" I had fond memories of spending summer weekends up here with Travis when we were teens, but hadn't been back in a few years.

"It's the most completely private place I could think of. No one but my family knows about it." Travis pulled into the driveway, parking the car in front of the garage.

I jumped out of the car, breathing in the fresh country air. Closing my eyes, I tilted my head back and let the sun soak in. *I love it here.*

A shadow passed in front of me, blocking the glorious sun. I peeked out under my eyelashes to see Travis standing in front of me with a beaming smile.

"What? Why are you looking at me like that?" I asked, crossing my arms over my chest.

"I just haven't seen you this relaxed in months." He stepped close to me, pinning me against the car.

I tilted my face up to his, "Well, that's probably because I've been trapped in the nut house with a bunch of crazy girls."

He laughed and inched closer to me. "I really want to kiss you right now."

"Are you kissing the other girls?"

Travis shook his head. "Only you," he whispered, leaning in closer.

I stood up on my tiptoes ready to close the distance, when the front door slammed open and a voice called out, "Are you two just going to stand there and stare at each other, or are you going to come in?"

I whipped around recognizing the voice. "Shut up!" I squealed, pushing Travis back lightly and ducking under his arm. I ran up the steps into the waiting arms of Travis' mom.

"Kathy, what are you doing here?" I asked hugging her tightly. Honestly I didn't care why she was here, I was just incredibly happy to see her.

"Travis called me, said it might help you relax a little if you were able to talk to someone from the outside world," she said while patting my back. She held me out in her arms, looking me up and down. "You still look the same, but what are you wearing? Athletic clothes?"

I laughed and looked down at myself. I was wearing my typical running clothes as of late—capri running pants, tank top and running shoes.

"Um, yeah. I may have taken up running just to get away from the girls for a while," I said, following her into the house.

"Liar," Travis said from behind me. "You took up running because you had to come up with some reason for leaving my house early in the morning."

"As I recall, you were the one who came up with the *brilliant* plan. I had no other choice." I took a seat at the kitchen table as Kathy poured us each a mug of coffee. "I could have just stayed at the main house at night." I glared over at Travis, since he was the one who asked me to come over every night.

"You don't have to agree!" He laughed. He sat at the table and started taking off his boot.

"Yeah right. If I don't agree to come over, you'll pout for hours and then start bombarding my phone with texts." I reminded him of the one night I just wanted to crawl under my covers and go to sleep, but Travis sent me over 50 texts begging me to come over—and that was before anything happened between us.

"Well, I can see the show hasn't changed you two at all." Kathy smiled at us as she took a seat at the table.

We quietly sipped our coffee, taking in the silence you can only experience in the middle of nowhere.

"So Riley, how do you like the girls that are left?" Kathy asked.

"Well… I like Taylor, she's a sweet girl. I misjudged Kara when the show first started; she's actually really fun to hang out with, though I really don't want to get on her bad side," I explained, glancing over at Travis wondering what he thought of those two. He kept his eyes on the table in front of him, ignoring my gaze.

"Anyway," I continued, "Nicki is the one person I *cannot* stand. She's obnoxious, self-centered and honestly, I'm pretty sure she's a pampered little princess where she lives. For the life of me, I can't understand why she is still here— aside from the fact that she is Travis' usual type."

Both Kathy and I turned to glare at Travis when I finished, only to find him glaring back at me.

"I don't have a type!" Travis exclaimed, setting down his mug hard enough for coffee to slosh over the edge.

"Sure you don't. We've only witnessed the trail of girls you've *dated*. They are all the same; tall, blond, heavily made up, obnoxious, self-centered, greedy, rude, only after you for the fame and money, dull, slu…" I trailed off as Travis stood to interrupt me.

"God, you make it sound like I am such a horrible person for seeing those girls. If you had an issue with it, why didn't you bring it up before, Riley?" He stormed out the door, slamming it behind him. I saw him cross in front of the window and take a trail into the woods.

"Hmmm, what did I say?" I asked his mom.

"The truth. Travis just never noticed the girls were like that. And he never knew you actually cared about it. I think hearing you describe the women he's dated made him view it from your eyes, and it hurt him. I can't imagine how you put up with it for all those years," she said, reaching out to grasp my hand.

"We were just friends, I had no reason to care who he dated."

"I think, deep down, Travis has always harbored feelings for you. He hated it when you would see that Milo guy. He was always so jealous when you would leave for a date…of course, he wouldn't say he was jealous, but a mother knows." Kathy smiled, squeezing my hand. "This show has opened your eyes to each other, which I am so grateful for, but I think it also scares Travis. He probably thinks he isn't good enough for you."

"What the heck? I've known him forever! I've known everything that goes on behind those closed doors. I don't care! It's in the past," I said, standing up and pacing the kitchen.

"I know that sweetie. Travis is just scared. Go. Talk to him." Kathy stood too, pushing me towards the door.

"But I just got here, I want to talk to you," I mumbled as Kathy turned me in her arms to give me a hug.

"I know, but we'll have time to talk another day. Besides, I have to get going." Kathy grabbed her purse and followed me out the front door. She waved as she headed to the garage. I waved back and turned towards the woods.

"Hope he didn't get lost," I grumbled as I headed towards the trail I saw Travis take.

I walked for a few minutes when I came to a small stream that flowed through the woods, signaling the end of the Grayson's property. Now I had a choice, I could take the trail left or right.

Great. Where did Travis go?

I turned left and saw Travis sitting at the base of a huge oak tree, staring out at the creek.

"Hey," I said, approaching him slowly, unsure of his mood.

"Hey," he replied without glancing up at me.

Well, at least he's talking to me.

I slid down the tree, settling myself next to him, not knowing what to say to him, so I just stared at the creek too. We both stayed quiet for a few minutes, listening to the creek trickle by and the sounds of woodland life.

"Why didn't you ever tell me what you thought of the girls I dated?" Travis quietly asked.

"Trav, I'm pretty sure I have mentioned it to you. You just never listened," I stated the truth, even though I was sure it would cause another argument.

"You've mentioned that you didn't like a few of them. But you mostly just kept your thoughts to yourself."

"I don't know what you want me to say, Travis. We were friends, it's not like I had a whole lot of right to stick my nose in your personal life. Whenever I did mention I didn't like the girl you were seeing, you ignored me anyway. You made it clear you were going to do what you wanted regardless of what I thought." I glanced over at him.

"I never realized what you really thought of them. It makes me sound like the biggest douche that I've only dated women like that." Travis sighed.

"Trav, I don't care about the women you've dated in the past. I knew none of them were going to stick around for the long haul, so it never really mattered," I said while I placed my hand gently on his knee.

"That's why you hate Nicki so much?" he asked. He gave my hand a small squeeze.

"I'm not sure who Nicki is when she is alone with you, but yes, she is exactly like all the other women you've dated. I've been trying to tell you that from the beginning."

"Jim was the one who wanted her around for a while, believing the ratings would go up with her added drama. But the more I've gotten to know her, the more I want her to stay for a while. I don't know. Maybe I'm just so used to my *type* that I can't navigate away so quickly." Travis glanced over at me and waited for my reaction.

Leaning my head back against the tree, I thought for a moment before replying. "I can understand that. You've been dating the same type for so long, it's hard to break the cycle. That's why I thought I was here, to help you move forward. But if you want to keep her for a while…do what you need to do."

"And Taylor? You actually like her?" Travis asked.

"I do like Taylor. She is a sweet girl. But she's also adventurous, which I know you would want in a girl." It felt awkward pumping Taylor up, but honestly, if it was between Nicki and Taylor, I'd root for Taylor all day, every day.

"And Kara?" he asked.

"Crap, Kara is like the female version of you. You two would be perfect for each other, except you'd kill each other after spending too much time together." I laughed just thinking about it.

"She is really fun to be around." Travis agreed.

"Yeah, she would fit great on your friends list."

"I'm glad I finally know where you stand. And I'm sorry the show isn't exactly what you signed up for," Travis said with a grin.

"Yeah, I wasn't expecting to actually want to be in the running for the finale," I muttered. I hoped I didn't sound too jealous.

Travis turned and cupped my face in his hands. "Riles, it'll be you at the end."

My heart skipped a beat at his words. I'll be honest, I had been worried he was going to change his mind and choose one of the other girls. Even though I've known him for so long, I can still never seem to figure Travis out.

"I'll be waiting." I breathed, my heart beating twice as fast as normal.

Travis leaned in and whispered, "Thank you" against my lips, before gently placing a kiss there.

I wrapped my arms around his neck, pulling him closer to me, and letting him deepen the kiss. I sighed and opened my mouth to him, tasting the coffee he had earlier.

Who knew kissing your best friend could be so amazing?

Chapter Twenty Four

All too quickly we were back in the car on the way to the house. Travis had told Jim the appointment would only last for about two hours, and we were now pushing three. Travis also mentioned he had an individual date with Kara later that day, which meant I would be spending my day with Nicki and Taylor.

Maybe Taylor and I could somehow hide out from Nicki all day. It would have been great if we could go off the property.

Ugh, it's going to be the day from hell.

Once we got back to the guest house, Travis jumped into the shower to get ready for his date, and I took off down the path towards the beach. I slowly made my way back to the house, trying to delay the inevitable. I climbed the stairs and saw Taylor lounging by the pool. She glanced up when she heard me.

"Hey girl. That was a long run today." She threw her arm over her eyes, shading them from the sun.

"Yeah, I felt really good so I just kept on going." I lied, walking past her. "I'm going to throw on my suit and I'll join you, okay?"

"Sure! Kara has a one-on-one with Travis today and nothing else is planned, so we pretty much are fending for ourselves," Taylor said, relaxing back into the lounge chair.

"Hopefully Nicki will stay indoors today," I grumbled. Taylor's laugh followed me to the door.

I quickly threw on my swimsuit, tossed a few essentials in my beach bag and headed back down to the pool. I pulled up a chair next to Taylor, adjusted the seat back, and threw my sunglasses on.

"It's beautiful out today," I said, closing my eyes and relaxing into the seat.

Taylor sighed, but said nothing.

We lounged around and in the pool all afternoon. Kara poked her head out to say goodbye about an hour ago and Nicki had yet to be seen.

Just as Taylor and I were discussing what we wanted for dinner, Nicki came out of the house and sauntered over to us with a wicked grin on her face.

She plopped down in the chair next to me, kicking her sandals off and lying back in the sun. She kept glancing over at me every few seconds.

I was tempted to ask if she had developed a twitch, but trying to play nice, I just sighed and asked, "What do you want, Nicki?"

"Oh, Riley, I didn't see you there," Nicki said, turning her head to fully take me in.

"Could you just get to the point and then scurry away?" I asked as I rolled my eyes. Did she have to be so oblivious that we didn't want her here?

"Yeah Nicki, you're ruining the mood out here," Taylor said from the other side of me. I laughed and wanted to reach over and high five Taylor for the slam on Nicki.

"No one was talking to you, *Taylor*," Nicki snarled in her direction.

Taylor just snorted and waved her hand dismissively in Nicki's direction.

Whoa! When did Taylor start fighting back?

"So anyway, Riley, you will never believe what I heard this morning," Nicki continued in a lower voice.

"And I'm sure I don't really care," I said, turning back to stare at the sky. It was much better to look at than Nicki.

"Oh, I'm sure you will care when I tell you," Nicki whispered conspiratorially.

I sighed and sat up, turning my body to face her. So much for her going away quickly and quietly. "You don't have to beat around the bush Nicki. Just tell me what you obviously came out here to say."

"I heard that one of the girls here is Travis' best friend." She sat up and turned, staring me straight in the eye.

Her comment got Taylor's attention and I heard her shuffle around behind me, then felt her sit down next to me.

"Really? That's crazy!" Taylor said, glancing between the two of us.

"Does it really matter?" I asked coolly, though inside I was freaking out. This wasn't supposed to happen. I was supposed to go undetected. I wondered who on the crew had a loud mouth.

"Of course it matters, *Riley*. These two had a deep connection prior to the show, and apparently they stepped out of the friend zone when they got here." Nicki continued to stare at me, and I squirmed under her gaze.

Seriously, who the hell had the big mouth?

I was pretty sure I was going to go kick his ass.

"It matters because if they have the connection I've heard about, then the rest of us are screwed. There is no way he's going to choose one of us in the end," Nicki continued with a sly smile on her face.

"Yeah, that does put a damper on things," Taylor muttered next to me.

"Travis is a big boy, Nicki. He decides who stays and who goes," I said indifferently.

Nicki rolled her icy blue eyes. "Cut the crap Riley. I don't know how you managed to get on the show, but I'm not letting your history with Travis destroy my chance with him."

Taylor gasped at Nicki's announcement. "Wow, everything makes so much sense now."

"What does?" I asked, sitting up straighter, ready to bolt.

"Whenever we were on group dates, you always knew what Travis was going to take us to do. And you had already done everything. It makes sense if you were his best friend, you would have done the stuff with him. Plus, I've also seen the looks that pass between you two. I always thought he just really liked you, but now it makes sense. And when we were playing truth or dare, he sat so close to you, and kept his hand on your leg all night," she said sadly.

Well, how the hell did she know that?!

"But why didn't you tell me?" Taylor asked, glancing at me with sad eyes.

I groaned and glanced at the camera crew surrounding us. I spotted Jim standing just behind one of the guys and he nodded his head slightly, giving me the go-ahead to tell these two why I was here.

"None of the girls were supposed to know about me. Travis asked me to come on the show to help him decide. We've done everything together, so it made sense. I wasn't happy that I actually had to *be* on the show, but the producers thought it was the only way I could get information on you guys to hand back over to Travis." I told this to Taylor, not really caring what Nicki thought of me. But I really didn't want Taylor to start hating me too.

"You gave him information on us?" she asked quietly.

"No, not really. He would basically ask me who I liked and who I didn't and why. I would tell him, but he would end up making his own decisions in the end," I explained.

Nicki snorted, "Yeah right."

"Oh, you should really believe that he makes his own choices, Nicki. Because if he listened to me, you would have been gone the first freaking night." I snapped at her and Taylor chuckled.

"And look at that. I'm still here. He still wants me here. What does that say to you?" Nicki laughed at me.

"It says the producers wanted you here until the top five, because you added drama." I leaned forward, getting close to her face. "But believe me, you will never end up with Travis at the end. He's had enough of your kind. He's ready to move on."

"Whatever Riley. One way or another, you are going home before me." She sneered at me. "You will not be in the top two. You do not get to *win* Travis." With that she hopped off the chair and strolled back into the house.

Taylor and I watched her walk away, before Taylor headed back to her chair and I leaned back against mine.

"So, did you two really become more than friends?" Taylor asked glancing over at me.

"We did. I honestly never thought of him that way, but somehow during the course of this show, things changed," I said looking over at her.

"That's so…romantic." She sighed. "And it really sucks for me."

"You aren't mad at me for...being who I am?" I was shocked she didn't seem pissed, but very grateful she wasn't.

"Of course I'm not. I understand why you did it. And you weren't allowed to tell anyone. You can't help your feelings. I didn't hate you before when I just thought you were another girl after Travis, why would I hate you now when I *know* you are another girl after Travis?" She laughed.

I smiled over at her, glad the secret was now out and I didn't have to cover my tracks anymore. And I was glad Taylor was cool with the whole thing. Oddly enough, she had become a good friend during my stay here, and I really didn't want to lose that friendship when the truth got out. Maybe it was better she found out this way, instead of her watching it when the show aired. At least she heard it from me—well technically from Nicki, but does she really count?

"I think it's adorable that you and Travis figured out how you felt about each other on the show. It would be wonderful to fall in love with my best friend...if I had a guy best friend." She chuckled and turned to face me. "I'm happy for you Riley."

"Um, the show isn't over. He could pick anyone!" I said, not wanting her to jump to conclusions.

"Uh huh. Whatever you say, Riley. He'd be dumb not to pick you." She waved her hand through the air.

"But...what about you?"

"I'll be fine. There are many other guys out there." She sat up and leaned close to me. "Does Travis have any brothers?"

I laughed loudly. "As a matter of fact he does. He has two older, very single ones."

"Well, there's still hope for me yet." Taylor chuckled and sank back into the chair.

Chapter Twenty Five

Later that night, I quickly made my way down the path to the guest house. Since everyone knew my secret, I was no longer worried about people seeing me go to Travis' place, but I still didn't want to get cornered by Nicki. Or even Kara at this point. I was thrilled by how Taylor reacted to the announcement, but Kara wasn't so accepting. In fact, she was pissed. She was back to that person I thought she was the very first night—a complete bitch.

Nicki had cornered Kara no more than two seconds after she got home from her date with Travis, to tell her the news. Kara's face went from a beaming smile, to a death glare in two point five seconds. It was not fun being on the receiving end of that.

I glanced up as I approached the guest house, and stopped in my tracks. Jim was standing outside the front door, looking as if he was expecting me.

"Riley, I figured you'd be coming over," he said as he held the door open for me.

"Um, yeah. I thought I should talk to Travis about what went on at the house today." I entered the house to see Travis sitting at the kitchen table.

"Hey Riles." He looked up at me warily.

"What's going on?" I asked taking a seat next to Travis.

Travis and Jim exchanged looks, before Jim explained, "Nicki is on the warpath. She is demanding that you get kicked off the show. She is saying you attacked her after she told you she knew who you were."

I stared at them, choking on my laugh. "Are you serious?! There are cameras all over the house!"

"She said you followed her into her bedroom." Jim added.

I looked between the two of them exasperated. Were they really going to take Nicki's word on this? How could they not know I would never be alone with her, ever?

"She is crazy. You two know I wouldn't do something like that!"

"We have people going through the video feed right now, trying to locate you during the time Nicki said you attacked her," Jim said calmly.

"Travis, you believe me, don't you?" I asked, since he had been quiet so far. He had to believe me. He's known me forever, and he knows I don't get catty like that. And I swear if he was about to take Nicki's side, I would walk. I couldn't deal with that crap.

"She had a bruise on her upper arm, where she said you slammed her into the door frame," Travis said, barely glancing at me.

"You mean the bruise on her upper left arm? The same place where she fell into the bar last week?" I asked, knowing for a fact that had been documented. Travis just shrugged.

That little shit believed her.

"She is delusional. She is absolutely insane," I yelled, standing up and pacing the kitchen.

"Again, we have the crew working on it right now to find out where you were. Obviously no one here believes you did this. She just wants you off the show. I'm not sure how the bruise occurred, but I wouldn't put it past her to have done it to herself," Jim said as he stood and walked over to me, placing his hands on my shoulder. "We'll figure this out Riley."

"Yeah. But this won't be the end of Nicki's wrath, she's bound to make my life a living hell until this show is over." Travis seemed to ignore what I said and laid his head down on the table. I glanced over at Jim, who just shrugged his shoulders.

"You're seriously doubting me, aren't you?" I asked Travis, as I leaned back against the counter to brace myself.

"I just don't know Riley. She was upset, she came to me crying. Why would she do that?" Travis once again glanced up at me warily.

"She's acting Travis! Oh my... I'm not even going to have this conversation with you anymore," I yelled, storming to the door.

"Riley, just wait a minute," Jim said calmly from behind me. He grasped my elbow to prevent me from walking out the door. I stopped, but jerked my elbow out of his grasp, turning around to face the both of them.

"What? Oh wait, you know what? No. I don't care what you have to say. Soon enough you will find out the truth, I had nothing to do with any of this. Then what?" I narrowed my gaze on Travis. "You think I'm just going to forget all about this? I don't know if you really have changed, Travis."

I turned and walked out the door, quickly getting away from that crazy man. Maybe he and Nicki were perfect for each other after all.

***

The following day I sat next to Taylor on the living room couch, drinking my third cup of coffee. It had been a long night. Once I got home I paced my room for an hour, infuriated that Travis would believe Nicki over me. Then Jim came to my room, informing me the camera crew was able to confirm that I was nowhere near Nicki when she claimed I was. Which I had already told them twenty times. At least Jim had the decency to apologize, and inform me that Nicki had gotten a warning. If she ever pulled something like that again, she would be kicked off the show. Though that thought made me feel slightly better, I had tossed and turned in my bed all night long, waiting for my phone to buzz with an apology from Travis. It never came.

Now we were all in the living room, waiting to find out who got the individual date with Travis today. I knew very well it wasn't going to be me, and since Kara had a date just yesterday, it wouldn't be her either. I prayed it would be Taylor, so I wouldn't have to see that smug smile of Nicki's.

But I knew Nicki had yet to have a one-on-one date, so I was bracing myself for the worst. And my nightmare was confirmed when Nicki came sauntering into the room with the envelope in hand.

"It's for me." She practically purred. She tore the envelope open and started reading out loud. "Nicki, I haven't had a chance to be completely alone with you yet, so I planned a low-key date to get to know you better. Don't eat lunch, I'll have some with me. Be there at noon to pick you up. Travis." Nicki looked directly at me with her smug smile that I wanted to punch off her face.

"Looks like I win today." She sneered at me before turning and heading up the stairs to get ready.

"Ugh. Can you believe her?" Taylor asked, rolling her eyes in Nicki's direction.

"She has been determined to make my life a living hell since I first got here. It stepped up a notch when she found out who I really am. I'm not surprised at what she does anymore."

"But she's not going to win. Why would she think that?" Taylor asked again, looking at me confused.

"Because Travis doesn't know what he wants at this point. I told you that you still had a chance. Nicki is exactly what he always went for in the past. Why should that change now that we're here?" I drained my coffee and went to get a refill. Taylor followed me into the kitchen.

"You're serious aren't you?" She grabbed a glass from the cabinet and the pitcher of water out of the fridge, looking over at me as I filled my cup with coffee.

"Yep. Travis is confused. I don't know if the thought of dating his best friend is now starting to freak him out, or if he's just not ready to give up his previous lifestyle. I just don't know anymore," I said, walking over to her, sipping my coffee.

"That's so weird. I really thought he was crazy about you." Taylor sighed. We heard the doorbell and Nicki's high pitch giggle, alerting us that Travis was here to pick her up.

"You may be right about the crazy part," I grumbled into my cup.

I retreated to my room shortly after Nicki left with Travis. I thought about getting a nap in, but realized that wasn't going to be an option once my head hit the pillow and my brain was still flying at a thousand thoughts per second.

Guess I shouldn't have had that fourth cup of coffee.

I reached in the bedside table and grabbed my phone. Maybe Kathy would be open to listening to me bitch about her son. I flicked on the screen and saw a text from Travis, sent just before noon.

Trav: Always you.

That was all. Was that a form of an apology? Why do his actions contradict everything he says?

Gah, could he be any more confusing?

I grabbed one of the books off my nightstand and walked over to the window seat. If I couldn't take my mind off Travis and his date by sleeping, maybe reading about someone else's life would help.

I sat back in the window seat, staring out at Lake Michigan. I couldn't believe Travis wanted an alone date with Nicki. I just couldn't believe he would do a complete 180 after everything we talked about yesterday. The only thing I could think is that this is adding an extra layer of drama to the show, and the producers think the ratings are going to skyrocket. *This is getting ridiculous.* I don't care how high the ratings are going to be—messing with people's lives is just wrong. I signed on so I could point Travis in the right direction. Nicki was *not* in that direction.

Sighing, I glanced down at the book in my lap, and caught movement out of the corner of my eye. I looked back out the window and saw Travis and Nicki heading down to the lake with a picnic basket. As much as I wanted to turn away and not watch the fiasco that the date was sure to be, I craned my head to see more of them.

Nicki kept touching Travis' arms and back, giggling hysterically at whatever Travis was saying. He spread out the blanket and was placing the basket on top, when Nicki jumped on his back. Travis twirled her around as she clung to his back, before lightly dropping her off. They stood, looking out at the lake and Nicki stepped closer to Travis, trying to cuddle into him. I blinked and rubbed my eyes to make sure I was seeing it correctly.

Yep, Travis had moved his hand to the small of her back, and Nicki was cuddling right into him. No, I couldn't watch this anymore.

Just when I was starting to turn away from the window, Nicki caught my eye again and then she stood on her toes and kissed Travis smack on the lips. It was quick and you could tell Travis wasn't expecting it, as he backed up slightly and stared down at her.

"Please don't do it. Please don't do it," I chanted under my breath.

I watched, unblinking, as Travis moved his hands to either side of Nicki's head. I saw his lips move as he said something to her, then she launched forward and attacked his lips again. Nicki grabbed his shirt with one hand, and tangled her other hand in his hair, while he kept his hands locked on her face.

My heart dropped. Tears formed in my eyes, and I finally managed to turn away from the window.

What was he doing? Why was he kissing her? Doesn't he know he's standing on the beach in full view of everyone in the house? Doesn't he know what kissing Nicki would do to me? It felt like my heart had just been ripped out of my chest and stomped on, over and over again.

I clutched at my chest, willing the pain to go away. Against my better judgment I glanced out the window again. Nicki had her arms wrapped around Travis' neck and her head was tilted back as she laughed at whatever Travis was saying to her. His hands were now gripped on her upper arms and he stared intensely at her.

I turned away from the window, tears now falling down my face. Slowly, I crawled onto the bed, curling up into a fetal position.

"This can't be happening," I muttered over and over again. My best friend was out there making out with the enemy, not giving a damn about me.

How can he do this? How can he throw whatever we had right out the window?

Nicki had declared war over Travis, and right now it felt like she was going to win.

Chapter Twenty Six

I'm not sure how, but I managed to fall asleep for a while. I woke up to a dark room and my stomach grumbling. Rolling onto my back, I stretched out, letting my muscles adjust to the new position. Leaning my neck to the side, I glanced at the clock—7:30. My stomach rumbled again, reminding me I had put nothing but coffee in it all day. I climbed off the bed, slowly shuffling downstairs to find something to eat. I got to the bottom step of the kitchen stairs, when I heard her voice coming from just outside the kitchen doorway.

"Oh, it was so *hot*! Not the best kiss I've ever had, but I can see why Riley kept him hidden." Nicki laughed loudly, entering the kitchen. She was followed in by Kara.

That two timing bitch Kara.

I was frozen at the foot of the stairs when Nicki's gaze zeroed in on me.

"Riley, there you are. Did you happen to hear how my date went?" She didn't wait for my response before continuing, "Oh wait, that's right, you *saw* how it went."

Holy shit, she planned the whole thing!

I could do nothing but stare at her. I knew she was conniving, but I never thought she could come up with something like this.

"What? You have nothing to say?" She pierced me with her ice cold eyes, her lips curled into a snarl.

"You planned it. You positioned yourself in that exact spot, knowing I would see you." I wanted to be in awe of her abilities, but really, I just wanted to rip her head off.

"Ding-ding. Give Riley a prize." She laughed in my face. "You gave me the ammunition I needed when you told me the only girls Travis dated were like me. I knew if I got him alone, all I had to do was flirt a little and he'd play right into my hands. Which he did…and more."

That little…

I launched at Nicki, but was quickly yanked back by Taylor. I never even saw her come into the kitchen.

"She tried to attack me! You all saw it!" Nicki screamed loudly.

"Shut up, Nicki. She didn't touch you. You can't do anything about it," Taylor hissed at her. "Plus, you provoked her. Honestly, I have it in me to let her go so she can finish what she wants to do."

"Yeah Nicki, as pissed at I am to know who Riley really is, you stooped to a whole new level today," said Kara, finally chiming in.

"Oh please, like none of you would have taken the chance when the opportunity came." Nicki rolled her eyes.

"Please let him eliminate you tonight. I'm so tired of your drama," Taylor said, her annoyance clear in her voice.

Nicki whipped her head to glare at Taylor and was probably about to say something bitchy, like usual, but we were interrupted when Jim walked into the kitchen.

"Ladies, you're needed in the living room for the elimination." He told us, holding his arm out, gesturing to the living room. I followed the girls out of the room, my stomach growling loudly. So much for getting something to eat, instead I got to deal with the wrath of Nicki.

We all found our spots in front of the window and waited quietly while Tessa and Travis walked in. Tessa set the box of bracelets on the table, opening it to reveal that they were burnt orange this time.

"We're entering the final week here, ladies. By the end of the night, there will only be three of you left vying for Travis' heart," Tessa said, smiling at us. "So, Travis, the floor is yours."

Travis walked up to the table, and picked up a bracelet. He rubbed it through his fingers, twirling it over and over. He looked up at us, moving his gaze to each one of us. When he landed on me, he winked.

He had the balls to wink at me?!

Did he seriously not know that I would find out he kissed Nicki? Did he think I didn't care? Seriously, I was beginning to think I should have him committed.

"Well, the secret is out now. Everyone knows that my best friend has been here since the beginning. Originally she was just supposed to be here until the top five, but things have changed, and I'd like for her to stay even longer," he said holding the bracelet up and giving me his sexy grin.

Why does he still have to be so attractive?!

"So, Riles, you want this bracelet?" he asked grinning at me.

I should say no. I should honestly say no and just walk the hell out.

But I felt my feet moving toward Travis. I glanced up at him giving him a tiny smile as he slid the bracelet on my wrist. He leaned in to hug me and I tensed slightly.

"Come over tonight?" he whispered in my ear. I backed out of his grip and laughed.

"Probably not," I said and turned to walk back to my spot.

Why was he acting like nothing happened today? Was he seriously that big of a player and I had just never noticed it? I mean, I was well aware of how he was with girls before the show and maybe I was naive enough to think he would settle down with me. I knew Nicki had planned this all to get to me, but that didn't mean Travis needed to play along—but he did. And that hurt.

Preoccupied with my thoughts, I vaguely caught that Kara was the one being sent home before we were released from the clutches of Tessa. I quickly tried to make my way out of the room, deciding to head through the kitchen and up that staircase instead of the main one, so I could hopefully avoid Nicki and maybe even grab something to eat. My stomach hadn't let me forget I was hungry. I grabbed an apple, some cheese and water out of the fridge and turned to the staircase. I had my head down, focusing on the food, so I didn't notice the body standing there, until I bumped into a solid form. I stumbled back, before he could grab me and I found myself looking up into Travis' face.

"What do you want?" I hissed angrily. I didn't want to deal with him right now. I still wasn't sure if I was going to bite his head off or break down into tears.

"Why don't you want to come over?" he questioned, trying to touch my face.

I backed up slightly out of his reach.

"Riles, what is going on?" He seemed worried, which just pissed me off even more.

"If you think *really* hard, I'm pretty sure you can figure out what is wrong," I said. I tried to glare at him, but my vision was starting to get fuzzy from the tears forming.

Travis just stared at me with a confused look on his face, so I brushed past him, taking the stairs two at a time. I got jerked to a stop when I was half way up when Travis grabbed my wrist.

"You need to tell me what is wrong, so I can fix it." He pleaded in a whisper. I pulled out of his grasp and turned to look at him.

Seriously, he's an idiot!

"You know, when you want to have a private date on the beach, you should really make sure it's in a more secluded area so people can't see you from their bedroom window," I spat out at him.

Travis visibly paled and opened his mouth to say something, but I turned and ran up the rest of the stairs and into my room before he could get a word out. I threw the lock on my door as soon as I entered. I figured he wouldn't have the balls to come to my room, even though Nicki and Taylor knew who I was. But if he did shock me and come up here, I wanted to make it clear that I had nothing to say to him.

I crawled to the middle of the bed, munching my apple and filling my stomach with much needed food. It had been the most exhausting day I'd had in years. I didn't know what to feel anymore. Should I be pissed? Upset? Happy I am seeing Travis' true colors? So many emotions were coursing through me and I had no idea what to do with them.

A few tears slipped down my cheeks and I groaned, swiping them away. As much as my brain was telling me to hate Travis and walk away, my heart still loved the man.

After I finished the small amount of food I had grabbed, my stomach was content enough for me to fall asleep. I slept soundly for a few hours before being awoken by a quiet knock on my door. I glanced at the clock noticing it was a little after midnight.

Who would be knocking at this time?

My heart skipped a beat when a picture of Travis entered my mind, but quickly turned to pain when I remembered what had happened down on the beach. Plus, I still didn't believe he would try to sneak up here.

I cracked open the door and saw Jim peering back at me.

"Riley, may I come in?" he asked, though I wasn't sure why, considering he was going to come in regardless.

I stepped back and opened the door for him to come in, then closed it halfway. Didn't need Nicki thinking there was something going on between Jim and me.

"What's up Jim?" I asked rubbing my eyes.

"You need to go see Travis," he said, stating it as a command instead of a suggestion.

"Like hell I do." I snorted at him. Were these people crazy? I wasn't going anywhere near him, unless he wanted to be kicked in the balls.

"Riley, listen—" Jim started.

"No, you listen. And you can tell Travis exactly what I'm telling you. I can't be alone with him again until he can make up his damn mind. I'm tired of this." I sat at the edge of my bed. "I'm just so tired of this, Jim."

"Riley, I know this isn't what you bargained for when you signed on, but you can't give up on Travis." Jim stood in front of me, lightly touching my shoulder.

I glanced up and gave him a small smile, "I'm not giving up on him. You have no idea how much I'm kicking myself for saying that, but I just can't give up on him. But I can't be placed second to the rest of the girls anymore. My heart physically cannot take it."

"You know there is still a show going on, right?" Jim asked softly.

Of course I did, what the hell did he think?!

"Yes, obviously. And I realize he can't pick one girl right now, when there are still three of us left. I know he has to show interest in the other girls, but my heart cannot take it. I cannot take seeing him kiss that bitch," I hissed through my teeth.

"So what do you want to do?"

"I told you. I won't be alone with him until he can make up his mind. No late night house visits, no individual dates, no being freaking cornered in the kitchen. I do not want to be around him right now." I blinked back the tears that were starting to well up in my eyes again.

"Okay. I'll let Travis know. I hope we can work something out," Jim said before letting himself out of my room and closing the door gently behind him.

Chapter Twenty Seven

I once again found myself sitting on the sofa in the living room next to Taylor, as Nicki went to answer the door and receive what we figured would be the final date envelopes.

"Tough night?" Taylor asked, eying my ridiculously large cup of coffee.

"You have no idea." I sighed and leaned my head back against the couch. After Jim left, I once again wasn't able to fall asleep. Travis sent me a few texts, begging me to come over and had even gotten his mom to send me a text saying I should talk to him. I had written and deleted so many texts to Travis throughout the night, ranging from me cussing him out, to me telling him I loved him. Ugh.

I loved him. That makes everything so much more complicated!

I even found myself standing by the outside door of the kitchen, hand on the handle. All I'd had to do was make the decision to turn the knob and run to the guest house, but I forced myself to retreat back to my room instead.

I opened my eyes when I heard Nicki come clomping back into the room with three envelopes in her hand. Without saying a word, she set two envelopes on the coffee table and then turned and ran up the stairs, clutching hers in her hand. Taylor leaned forward and grabbed the two off the table, flipping them over and reading the names.

"One for me. One for you," she said, handing me the one with my name written on the front. I watched as she opened hers and read it.

"It says the final dates are today. Each of us are getting a meal and a block of time with Travis. I apparently have lunch and the afternoon spot," Taylor said, glancing up at me, noticing that I still hadn't touched my envelope. "I'm assuming Nicki had the morning by the way she took off like that... Are you going to open yours?" Taylor pointed to the note on my lap.

Probably not. I shrugged, not really caring what Travis had to say. It wasn't like I was actually going to go on the date with him anyway. Taylor patted my knee before getting up from the couch.

"I'll let you have some space," she said sadly, before heading up to her room.

I glanced down at the letter sitting on my lap. Part of me wanted to rip it open and see what Travis had to say. The other part of me wanted to throw it in the fireplace and watch it burn. In the end, the curiosity won out. I slid my finger under the flap, tearing open the envelope and pulling out the letter. Slowly I unfolded it and read:

Hey Doll - I know I've been an ass, and you have every reason to not want to see me anymore. But PLEASE come over for dinner tonight. I'll cook up something delicious—I know how much you love my cooking, and we can talk. This arguing and not talking thing is killing me. I miss you Doll. I need to see you. - Travis

I smiled at the letter. Travis knew me too well. He knew it would be hard for me to turn down his cooking, since he made my absolute favorite dish—chicken pesto linguine—to perfection. And he was right about the arguing and not talking; I may be mad at him, but it really was killing me to not talk to him. There is a point where you just miss someone so much that you just want it to be normal for a while—I was at that point. Just as I was deciding that I was going to go to Travis' and try my hardest to be civil and move forward, Nicki came bounding down the stairs, wearing the shortest summer dress I had ever seen. I didn't think it was possible, but she looked even more slutty than normal. This time I was very aware of what she was trying to do and I wasn't going to take the bait.

"Well I'm off for my breakfast date with Travis," Nicki said, breezing into the room. "I was thinking a few mimosas will get Travis loosened up and then he'll be putty in my hands."

Don't listen to her. She's just trying to provoke you.

I stood up and brushed past her, heading up to my room.

"Yeah, probably better that you're not here to see our greeting," Nicki called up after me.

Just keep moving.

I highly doubt Jim would be accepting if I were to punch Nicki in the face—even if she did deserve it. I ran into my room, yanking open the drawer that contained my phone. The drawer came tumbling out of the table, spilling its contents across the floor. I tossed some books aside and grabbed my phone, quickly sliding the screen to get to my messages. I pulled up Travis' name and typed as quickly as my fingers would go, praying he got my text before he met Nicki.

Me: I'll meet you tonight for dinner. PLEASE don't do anything with Nicki. Please!

I know I probably sounded desperate, but I was pretty sure I couldn't stand another Nicki make-out fest. I paced around the room with the phone gripped in my hand.

Please get it before your date. Please, please!

Yep, I was starting to sound like a crazy person. I heard Nicki loudly giggle from downstairs, and my heart dropped.

He didn't get it in time.

I slowly gathered up the things that had fallen on the floor when I had yanked the drawer out of the table. I put the drawer back into the bedside table and started filling it with the items I gathered. I was just about to place my phone back in behind a book, when I felt it buzz. My hand slammed against the top of the table as I yanked it out. I swiped at the screen and saw a new text from Travis.

> *Trav: I'll make your fav. And after what happened last time you think I'd be that stupid? I have my Nicki repellent on.*

I laughed loudly while my heart picked up speed. I wasn't crazy, he really didn't want Nicki. I really hoped he could deflect her moves today.

> *Me: Good to know. See you later.*

Just then the doorbell rang and I heard Nicki run to answer it.

"Oh Travis, I'm so glad we get to hang out this morning." She squealed loudly, probably for my benefit. I didn't hear anything else for a while, imagining the worst.

Don't go there, he said he wasn't going to do it, trust him.

"Nicki no. That's not happening," Travis said, interrupting the silence. Did he just push her off him? I was tempted to run to the stairs to see what had happened, but decided to put my trust in Travis.

I spent the rest of the morning lounging by the pool reading a book until Nicki came back. Then I quickly changed into my running gear and took off down the beach. I wasn't going to be stuck in the house alone with her for three plus hours, I really didn't want to hear her description of the date. So the best option was to run away from her. I jogged the beach three times and then simply sat and enjoyed the rushing waves of Lake Michigan.

I stayed there for another hour before heading back to the house to get ready for my *date*. I quickly showered and stood in front of my closet debating whether I wanted to look pretty or if I wanted to go my usual route of jeans and a t-shirt. I reached in to grab a shirt, when I caught my birthday dress out of the corner of my eye.

Oh, I suppose that will do.

I reached in and pulled it off the hanger, smiling as memories from that day flashed through my head. I threw it over my head and went to work with my hair. Working swiftly, I created a loose fishtail braid to the side and draped it over my shoulder. I applied a quick swipe of shimmery nude eyeshadow, applied some mascara and ran some balm across my lips.

Let's not get too fancy here; it was just dinner with Travis after all. Checking myself one last time in the mirror, before calling it good, I headed down into the kitchen.

I'd heard Taylor come home about an hour ago, so I figured I was good to go to Travis', even if I was a little early. I made my way down the path to the guest house, hoping the night would go smoothly. This stupid show had caused more fights between us than we'd ever had before—in fact, we never fought before this show. Oh, was I ever ready to be done with this show. If I could end it tonight and walk away with Travis, I would in a heartbeat.

I reached the guest house and saw Travis through the kitchen window, standing over the stove. He had the windows open so the amazing scent of pesto drifted through the night air. His hair was damp from a recent shower, but tousled perfectly. Travis turned around, probably heading to the fridge, when he stopped short and stared directly at me. He broke into a dazzling smile and walked to the door, throwing it open.

"You're here," he said, pulling me into a tight hug.

"I told you I was coming," I mumbled into his chest, tensing a little at his touch. I loved the fact that he was hugging me, but he was squeezing me so tightly I could barely get a breath in anymore. "Uh Travis... too tight."

Travis loosened his grip, but didn't let me out of the hug. I relaxed into him a little, wrapping my arms around his waist. This was perfect, just like before the show. Except that my heart was going crazy and those stupid butterflies showed up in my stomach. While my insides were going crazy, my body language told a different story. I knew I wasn't relaxed completely into his arms like I should be and when he ran his hand up and down my back, I tensed up. Eventually Travis backed out of the hug and pulled me into the house.

"I hope you're hungry. I've been slaving over the stove all day," Travis said, returning to the stove to add pasta to the pot of boiling water.

"I'm sure your previous dates loved just sitting here watching you cook for me," I replied sarcastically.

"They don't matter," Travis said waving his hand over his shoulder. Okay, so he was obviously trying here, it probably wasn't the best idea to say something snarky back to him like I wanted to.

I watched as he added the cooked pasta to the pan with the chicken and pesto and lightly mixed it together before twirling it onto the waiting plates. He placed a plate in front of me and another in his spot, slid a bowl of fresh garlic bread into the middle of the table, and then walked to the fridge.

"Wine or hard cider?"

"When have I ever been a wine person?" I asked raising my eyebrow in his direction. He should have known the answer before questioning me. I pressed my lips together, thinking he probably got me mixed up with one of the other girls.

"Right. That's right." Travis pulled two ciders out of the fridge and returned to the table, sitting down opposite me. He opened both drinks, then slid mine across the table to me. I took a long swig then dug into the pasta.

"Mmmm. This is so good!" I exclaimed through my mouthful of food.

"You always act surprised when you eat the food I cook. When are you just going to accept that I'm amazing?" Travis said before digging into his own plate.

"You forget the one time you gave me food poisoning." I groaned remembering when he had attempted to make sushi—let's just say the fish was not fresh.

"You would bring that up. That was years ago—and how was I supposed to know the fish wasn't fresh?" He laughed, surely recalling me hovering over the toilet the entire next day.

"I still have nightmares about it." I shuddered, cringing at the memory. I never wanted to feel that way again. "Can we not talk about food poisoning while I enjoy this delicious meal?" Travis nodded and we ate the rest of the meal in silence.

"That was so good," I said, pushing back the chair and gathering up the plates. "Thank you for making me dinner." I started filling the sink with soapy water.

"Just like old times." Travis came up next to me and started rinsing and drying the dishes I had washed. We worked quickly, getting the dishes done in short time. It really was just like old times—except he would constantly bump me or touch me, and tingles would run through my body. Each time he would 'accidentally' touch me, I would tense and jerk my hand away. Let's face it, I really wanted things to be normal between us, but I just couldn't forget that quickly what happened yesterday—or the previous days for that matter.

"Want to watch a movie?" Travis asked, standing with his hands in his pockets like he was trying to keep from touching me.

"Is that code for something else?" I questioned, remembering the last time we 'watched a movie'. He let out the most beautiful laugh and pulled me into the living room.

"No code. Just a movie. Or we could talk," he said placing his hands on my shoulders. "Riles, I'm so sor…"

"Don't." I cut him off, shrugging out of his grasp. "Don't apologize. I really just want to forget about it."

Travis stared at me like he wanted to say more, but eventually nodded before flipping through the movies. We had just agreed on one, when a knock came from the kitchen door.

"Who would be here?" Travis asked, more to himself than to me. "Be right back." He patted my leg before hopping off the couch and answering the door. I was attempting to get comfortable on the couch when I heard Jim.

"Look, I know you're in the middle of your date with Riley. But the three of us need to talk," he told Travis as he appeared in the doorway of the living room.

"Of course we do." I groaned as I stood up and followed them to the kitchen, each of us taking a seat at the table.

Well if this didn't feel familiar.

"I'm not going to beat around the bush here. You two need to work your issues out. The audience is not going to cheer for the two of you if you continue to push each other away." Jim was talking wildly to us with his hands.

"I thought that's what we were doing right now," Travis replied, obviously bewildered by Jim's statement.

"I know you two had a nice sit down meal. That was it. It was a meal between two friends. It wasn't a dinner one would expect two people who actually *liked* each other would have," Jim explained, looking directly at me.

I knew he was telling me this and not Travis. As hard as I was trying to pretend everything was okay between Travis and me, I knew I wasn't that great of an actor on the outside. I knew my body language was telling him to back off. I couldn't help it—I was still pissed at him for the whole Nicki thing. One day was not enough time to get over it.

"I have my issues worked out. Travis knows what he needs to do," I mumbled, twisting my hands in my lap. I really didn't want to start another fight with him, but by the look on his face, that was exactly where it was going.

"What do you want me to do Riles? Do you want me to end the show right now? Leave with you?" Travis pushed back from the table and stood up.

"I didn't say you needed to end the show right now. I just said you needed to figure your shit out. I'm tired of this Travis. I physically cannot watch you date these other girls anymore," I yelled back at him, remaining in my seat.

"I don't understand. You won't let me date other girls without being pissed. I *have* to date them because that is what this show is about! And I've told you time and time again that it is always going to be you at the end. When are you going to believe me?" Travis was pacing back and forth shaking his head at me. "But even still, I have to see this out until the end! I signed a contract. You know I don't break my contracts!"

"Travis! I didn't even want to be here. I never signed up to actually be in the running. *You* did that. You were the one who kissed me, who made his feelings clear for me, who put me smack dab in the middle of the show. You were the one who told me over and over not to worry about anything, and then you go off and make out with the remaining contestants! What the hell am I supposed to think? You made me freaking fall in love with you!" I stood and started pacing the kitchen. I glanced up at Travis who had stopped pacing and stared at me with his mouth agape.

"You love me?" he asked.

That was what he caught from my rant? Really?

"Trav, that is not really the point here." I was beyond frustrated with this conversation and just wanted to end it. "You know what? Do whatever the hell you want, you clearly aren't listening to me. Tomorrow there is an elimination right?" I glanced at Jim who gave a slight nod.

"There you go Travis, make it easy on everyone—eliminate me tomorrow." I started to move toward the door when Travis caught me by the arm.

"Is that what you want? You want to leave?" he asked, seriously confused. I shrugged out of his grasp and crossed my arms over my chest, rolling my eyes at him.

"Travis, I just want you. That's all. I don't want this drama, this game, I don't care about the final two—I just want *you*! But you seem confused about everything. And if you are that confused about it all, then I don't want to be here. I shouldn't be a second guess, Travis. You should know whether or not you want me." I stormed to the door, slipping on my sandals. "So do what you want. I'm done. I'm done playing this game. Do. What. You. Want," I yelled, before throwing the door open and running up to the main house.

Well this night turned out like shit.

Chapter Twenty Eight

Today was the first day since I've been here where I actually packed up my things before an elimination. Every other time I pretty much knew I was safe—tonight, I wasn't so sure. I tucked my phone into my purse and set it next to the bags on my bed. If I were to go home, someone from the crew would come up and grab my bags and load them in the SUV before it came around the front to pick me up. Or at least that was what we were told prior to the show starting.

To be honest, I wasn't even sure if I wanted to be here anymore. It wasn't that I didn't want to be with Travis, because I did, more than ever. But I just couldn't deal with this drama anymore. I wanted to be with Travis on my terms, away from the cameras and glaring eyes of the other contestants. But Travis was set on seeing things through to the end and I would have to accept that. Just like I would have to trust him when he kept telling me it was always going to be me at the end. And I was trying, but I knew Nicki's type, and she'd do anything in her power to get her claws in him and make him think twice. Then you have Taylor, who is the sweetest girl ever—I could see why Travis would be starting to fall for her. Whatever happened tonight, it would be a game changer, that's for sure.

I made my way down to the living room, knowing I had only two minutes to get there before Tessa and Travis were due to show up. I saw Nicki and Taylor standing in their spots in front of the wall of windows, so I quickly made my way to the only open spot, which was on Nicki's other side. *Of course they'd put the viper in the middle.*

"Took you long enough to get in here. I hope you're all packed up," Nicki whispered loudly in my direction. I just shook my head, rolled my eyes and tried my best to ignore her, even though my heart picked up speed at the thought of being eliminated.

Maybe I should find Travis and tell him what I said last night was crazy talk. I didn't really want to go home. I wanted to be there…with him. I was about to move from my spot to find him, when he and Tessa walked in the room. Tessa placed two golden yellow bracelets on the table and nodded to us.

"Ladies, you've made it this far! Congratulations! Tonight is a tough one as it'll be narrowed down to the final two and I know Travis has had a connection with each of you ladies." Tessa said with a smile. She turned to Travis, "Okay Travis, it's your turn."

"It's been a rough night, that's for sure." Travis started, picking up one of the bracelets. "So many decisions needed to be made and I truly hope I made the best ones." He looked up at us, holding each of our gazes for a moment, before looking back down at his hands and continuing, "With that said, this first bracelet is going to Taylor."

"Oh!" Taylor exclaimed. She glanced over at me before walking up to Travis. He slid the bracelet on her wrist and she gave him a light hug before moving back in line smiling over at me.

"Nicki and Riley, please come stand in front of Travis," Tessa told us, gesturing to the open space in front of them. I quickly glanced over at Taylor for some moral support and she winked, giving me the thumbs up. I smiled back at her before moving to stand in front of Travis. I kept my head down, afraid that if I looked Travis in the eyes, I'd see something I didn't want to see. I held my breath waiting for him to pick the final person. I'd be lying if I said I didn't care. Obviously I did. I wanted to stay, regardless of what I told him last night. I wanted to be with Travis, but I wasn't sure what he would do. This show had messed with his pretty head—and mine too.

I glanced up at his hand where the golden bracelet sat in his palm, then to his face where he was looking between the two of us.

"Travis, who is going to be your final choice?" Tessa asked from beside him.

I glanced back at Taylor, who was still giving me a beaming smile. I loved that she was rooting for me even though she knew who I was and my relationship with Travis. I gave her a small smile back before turning my attention to Travis.

"This last choice wasn't easy. It really did keep me up all night." He exhaled loudly, staring down at his hands.

Wasn't easy? Oh, this can't be good.

"I've come to know you, Nicki, quite well in the last few weeks. And Riles, well, you're my best friend." Travis closed his eyes taking a deep breath. "I think I've come up with a good plan that makes everyone happy, I just hope it doesn't blow up in my face."

What the hell is he talking about?!

"This last bracelet is going to Nicki," Travis said barely above a whisper.

I stared opened mouthed as Nicki sauntered up to Travis and planted a wet kiss on his lips. I blinked back the tears, barely registering that Travis had gently pushed Nicki back, before I was enveloped in Taylor's arms.

"Oh my God, I cannot believe he did that," she whispered in my ear, hugging me tightly.

I was thankful that Taylor was holding me—I felt like I was about to pass out. My chest physically started to hurt, making me reach between Taylor and myself to try and rub the pain away. Nope. Didn't work. The pain only intensified.

"Riley, are you okay?" Taylor held me at arm's length eying me up and down.

I stared at her trying to form some sort of word for how I felt. I'd never felt like this before. It felt like my entire world was ripped out from under me and my damn chest would not stop pounding.

"Sweetie, I honestly thought he was going to pick you—you two are made for each other." Taylor hugged me again.

"Clearly not." I choked out, willing myself not to cry. I would not leave this show like a blubbery mess.

"He's stupid. He'll come around," Taylor whispered to me, squeezing me tight before releasing me.

"I don't know if I can wait for that though," I whispered back.

Taylor just smiled at me sadly and nodded her head.

"I hope he picks you." My heart broke as I said those words to Taylor, giving her a small smile. I honestly did hope he picked her, now that I was out of the picture. As much as it killed me to say those words out loud, it would kill me more if he ended up with Nicki.

Maybe, just maybe we can salvage our friendship if he picks Taylor. But if he chooses Nicki at the end, it would be over completely.

Taylor pulled me into a hug as Travis started walking our way. "Honestly, I don't think he's going to choose either of us," she whispered in my ear. "I'm going to miss you so much. You have my number, use it okay?" She pulled away waiting for my response. I only got out a nod before Travis was next to us.

"Taylor, I'm sorry, but I have to escort Riley to the car now," Travis said gently.

Taylor nodded and started walking away, flashing the 'call me' sign and mouthing it, causing me to laugh.

"Riles, I…" Travis started, but I stormed away from him before he could finish. If he thought he was going to apologize for this crap, he was seriously out of his mind—which after picking Nicki, I was honestly considering he may very well be.

"Riley wait up." Travis jogged up to me trying to grab my hand.

I jerked away from him and walked out the front door, letting it swing closed behind me and hoping it smacked Travis in the face.

"Riley, I'm supposed to say goodbye. It's part of the show. And I need to explain to you why I did this. It's not what you think!" Travis said as I stood in the middle of the driveway glancing around for the car that would take me away.

"Riles, they have to take your stuff out to the SUV before it'll come around the front and pick you up. You still have about fifteen minutes left with me. Please, let me explain." Travis tried again, but I refused to acknowledge him.

I heard him huff before he stomped over to stand directly in front of me.

"Damnit Doll, would you talk to me?" he yelled, his voice cracking slightly.

"What do you want me to say Travis?" I shrugged. "Do you want me to say I'm glad I'm leaving because I hated this damn show? Did you want me to say I'm happy you kept Taylor? Did you want me to say that you broke my damn heart when you chose Nicki over me? Did you want me to say that looking at you right now is literally tearing me up inside? Because it's all true. I do hate this show, I'm glad cameras aren't going to be watching my every move anymore. I'm glad you decided to keep Taylor on, she's a great girl. I've never had a broken heart before, but I'm pretty sure this is what it feels like. And I *cannot* look at you without seeing the past fifteen years of our friendship being completely destroyed by that one choice you made. You made your choice. I'm not it. I'm going home—without you. It is killing me to look at you right now and it *will* kill me if you touch me. I just want to be alone and wait for the car, so I can get as far away from you and this house as I possibly can." I vaguely noticed the camera crew lined up around us getting this shot at every angle.

Great…Like I really wanted this documented.

"Riles, please." Travis reached out to touch me, but I backed out of his reach just as an SUV came pulling up behind the camera crew.

"Bye Travis," I whispered as I ran to the SUV, quickly hopping into the backseat and buckling myself in. The vehicle started to pull away and I took one last look at Travis. He had dropped down on the front stoop, his elbows on his knees and his head in his hands. He glanced up for a second when the SUV passed in front of him. It was enough for me to catch the pain etched on his face.

216 | CAYLIE MARCOE

Seeing him sitting like that with the defeated look as the SUV pulled out almost made me lose my composure, but, unsure if there was another camera in the car, I just leaned my head back against the headrest and closed my eyes, taking a deep breath to try and cleanse this night away.

I opened my eyes and glanced around the car. No one was here but me and the driver.

"There aren't any cameras in here, are there?" I asked once we pulled out of the driveway.

"No. There usually are, but we decided you've had enough cameras for a while." I was shocked when it was Jim who responded to me. I leaned forward and caught his eye in the rear-view mirror.

"I'm also going to assume you are not the person who usually drives the girls to the hotel."

"Riley, I didn't know this was going to happen," Jim explained softly.

I quickly brushed away a tear that had managed to escape and roll down my cheek. "It doesn't matter," I mumbled.

"Don't say that Riley. It's just you and me here. Last night after you left, I told Travis the game could be over. It was down to the final three, America is already rooting for you two so it just didn't matter anymore. We have the ratings, it's no big deal." Jim glanced up in the mirror as he explained this to me. "He said he'd keep the show going until the contract said it was done."

"That's Travis; he has to see things through."

"I don't know what this is about. I don't know what is running through his head here. It doesn't make sense." He was shaking his head like it was totally unbelievable to him too. "I've only known you two for a short time, but even I can see what the two of you have."

"Can we just please stop talking about this?" I asked quietly. I saw Jim nod his head then he reached over and turned the radio on.

We pulled up in front of a simple hotel. Jim stopped at a side door and got out of the car, pulling my bags out of the trunk. I climbed out to help him.

He pulled out a key card from his front pocket. "This is your room key, room 302. You are already checked in and don't worry about checking out tomorrow, someone from the crew will come and do it for you. Since the show is currently airing, we need you to stay in your room or in the shadows. Tomorrow there will be a car to take you home. Once home you'll need to lay low for a few days. We just need to make sure word hasn't gotten out that you were eliminated before the finale. Once you get the all clear, you can resume life as normal. Hang out with friends, go back to work…" Jim trailed off as I'm sure he remembered who I worked for. "I'm sorry Riley."

I held up my hand to stop him, "Don't worry about it. I understand what I need to do. Thanks for the ride Jim." I grabbed my bags from him and made my way to the side door. Sliding the key through the lock, I opened the door and propped it open with my leg as I gathered up my bags. I waved at Jim when he drove past and honked at me, before turning and heading up the stairs to my room for the night.

I was glad it was late when I fell onto the bed of the hotel room. I just wanted to curl up and sleep away this horrible day. Tomorrow I would be in my own bed, *completely* alone and right now, I wasn't sure if that made me happy or incredibly sad.

Chapter Twenty Nine

I tossed my mail onto the counter and turned to put the kettle on the stove to boil water for my coffee. I noticed the corner of a gossip magazine peeking out from behind some bills. My curiosity got the better of me as I brushed the bills aside and saw the full cover of the magazine. Travis was smiling back at me, with pictures of Taylor, Nicki and me in little boxes under him. The headline of *Freestyle Star Finds Love in an Unexpected Place* was positioned above Travis' head. They also had drawn a bunch of cutesy little hearts around my head, with *BFF* in one of the hearts.

Stupid gossip rags.

Of course they would play up the best friend part. From what I knew my elimination episode aired last week, with the finale airing tonight. The magazine had jumped the gun a little.

I pushed the magazine into the trash as the kettle started to whistle. I poured the water into my French press filled with coffee grounds and placed the top on to let the coffee steep. Reaching into the cookie jar for one of the cookies I made the other day, I headed into the living room to lounge on the couch.

Just as I sat down, I heard a knock on my door. Sighing, I set the cookie on the coffee table, stood, and walked slowly to the door. I glanced through the peephole then leaned my head against the door, not ready for the conversation I was sure was about to take place. Taking a deep breath, I opened the door.

"Hi Kathy." I held the door open for her to enter.

She smiled as she walked by me, setting her purse on the bench by the door and dropping her sweater over the top of it.

"Riley honey, how are you holding up?" She scooped me into a hug, rubbing my back like any mother would.

"Me? Oh…I'm fine." I backed away from the hug, turning my back on her and heading back to the couch so she couldn't see the truth in my eyes.

Because the truth was, I was anything but fine. My heart was still broken into a million pieces. The whole world had seen it happen last week on TV. And I hadn't spoken to my best friend in two months, aside from a few generic "Hi, how are you?" texts, which I never replied to. In fact, the last time I'd heard his voice was when I turned my back on him and ran to the SUV after he eliminated me on the show. I could still see his anguished look while he sat on the stoop outside the house after I got into the vehicle without letting him explain things.

Like he could have explained anything anyway.

But the worst part was whenever I closed my eyes, I could see Nicki after my elimination planting a kiss on him and giggling and smirking at me like she'd just won. It made me sick to my stomach every time.

So yeah, I was anything but fine. But I wasn't about to let Travis' mom know that. I plopped down on the couch, scooping the cookie off the table and stuffing it in my mouth before Kathy asked me something else. I glanced up at her and immediately knew it was the wrong move. Her eyes were full of sadness and pain of her own.

"Sweetie, I know you better than that." She sat right next to me, patting my knee.

Just that simple comment and touch caused tears to form in my eyes. I tried to blink them back, but failed and one rolled down my cheek.

"Oh Riley." Kathy wrapped her arms around me and pulled me into another hug rubbing her hands across my back.

This time I embraced the hug and buried my head in her shoulder, letting the sobs out that I had been holding in for the past two months. My whole body shook as I cried. I tried to keep the sobs from escaping my mouth by clenching my lips together, but a few would loudly escape, causing me to cry that much harder.

I cried for a while, letting Kathy rub my back and whisper calming words into my ear. Finally I took a deep breath and released it slowly before sitting up away from Kathy. She handed me a few tissues from the box behind the couch. I tried to smile at her and dabbed at my eyes and nose until I was sure I wasn't leaking anymore. I excused myself and went to the bathroom to splash some water on my face, leaning against the sink and looking into the mirror. My eyes were bloodshot and puffy. My face was all red and splotchy. My lips had teeth marks across them from trying to hold in my sobs. And water was dripping off my chin onto my shirt.

Yeah, I looked awesome.

I turned the cold water on and splashed my face again, before grabbing a towel and patting it dry. I headed to my room and quickly changed into a dry shirt before heading back to Kathy.

I paused in the kitchen and glanced at the clock. Only ten minutes had passed since I let Kathy in.

It definitely felt longer than that.

I saw my French press sitting on the counter. "Would you like some coffee?" I called to Kathy, my voice rough from the crying.

"If you want to make some, I wouldn't turn it down," Kathy replied, I could tell it was with a smile. That woman never turned down the offer of coffee.

"I had some brewing before you got here. It's still warm." I started to pour coffee into two mugs I grabbed from the cupboard. "Do you still take it with a splash of cream?"

"For the last thirty years!" She laughed from the living room.

I smiled and added a small amount of cream to her mug and a large glug to mine. I placed the mugs on a tray and grabbed a few more cookies from the jar, setting them on a small plate on the tray before carrying it out to the living room. I placed the tray on the coffee table and handed Kathy her coffee before taking mine and settling onto the couch next to her.

"So, what brings you here?" I asked, sipping my coffee.

It wasn't unusual for Kathy to come to my place out of the blue, but I hadn't heard from her since Travis eliminated me from the show. I didn't really think anything of it, since she was his mom and all, and if she was going to pick sides it was obviously going to be Travis'.

She took a sip of her coffee before answering. "I think it's about time you and Travis sit down and talk."

I shook my head, not sure I heard her right. "Why on Earth would I do that? You know what he did."

"I know, my son is a dumbass. But the show is over now, the finale is tonight, I'd like for you to come over to our place and watch it."

I could only stare at her. Was she out of her mind? Why would I subject myself to that kind of pain? I haven't watched any of the episodes on TV because I knew they would break my heart all over again. It was just too painful. I mean, not only had I lost my best friend, but I also lost the guy I was most definitely in love with.

"Is Travis going to be there?" It came out barely above a whisper.

Kathy nodded, staring at me over the rim of her coffee mug.

"And the girl he picked?" I choked out. Really, why would she do this to me? Was she secretly that heartless?

"Please come. You're family and we'd like you to be there." She avoided my question. *Not a good sign.*

"Does Travis want me there?" He kicked me off the show after all, and hadn't talked to me since even though I was well aware he had his phone with him and could have used it at any time, especially since the show had finished filming a little less than two months ago and he'd been home ever since. It was like I had been excommunicated from their family.

"I'm not sure he's completely aware of the plan, but I do know he wouldn't object to it." She finished her coffee and set the mug back on the tray staring intently at me.

"I don't know… I'll have to think about it." My eyes pleaded with her to just leave it at that.

"Okay, we'll be having dinner at five with the showing after." She smiled at me. "I'd really like for you to be there."

"I'll think about it," I muttered again, hoping this was the end of the discussion.

She settled back into the couch, "So what have you been doing for the last few weeks?"

She was downplaying it. She knew very well it had been two months since I was eliminated. Two months since I last spoke to Travis. Two months since she told me I should take a break from my job. What have I been doing? Going crazy out of my mind with boredom. I wanted my job back so I could at least do *something* with my days…and I could see Travis again.

"Oh, nothing too exciting. Lots of time on my hands with nothing exciting to do," I said, willing her to say something, anything about going back to work.

"Yes, I suppose you do have a lot of time on your hands. I think it's about time you come back to work."

"Thank goodness!" I sighed, "I've been going out of my mind trying to figure out who was stepping in as Travis' assistant. Did they field phone calls right, did they know the ins and outs of his day, did they know how he takes his coffee in the morning, and that you're not allowed to talk to him until he gets at least half of it in him?" I was rambling, I knew it, but I was excited at the idea of going back to work, even if it meant seeing Travis and dealing with painful memories. I guess I was ready to move forward, I missed my best friend and I wanted my job back. I looked up at Kathy who was staring at me smiling.

"Only you would know how to take care of my son so well," she said, standing. "I have to get going now to prepare dinner for tonight, are you coming over?"

"Yeah, I'll be there," I said, resigned to the fact that it needed to be done—I needed to rip the band-aid off and see Travis again, even if this was going to be the most painful way possible.

"Good, I'm so glad!" Kathy said pulling me into a hug. "Oh, and I was the one who took over your job for the last two months. Do you think I'd trust Travis in the hands of anyone but you?" She backed out of the hug, grinning at me, and headed out the door. "See you tonight!" she called over her shoulder, before I shut the door behind her.

I fell back onto my couch, picking up my now lukewarm coffee and taking a sip.

What had I just gotten myself into?

Had I really just agreed to have dinner and watch the finale of the show with Travis and, most likely, the girl he picked? I knew I needed to see Travis again, but there had to be a better way!

I had just picked up my phone to call Kathy and let her know I changed my mind, when it buzzed in my hand with an incoming text.

> Trav: Mom just told me you are coming over for dinner tonight. Can't wait to see you!

I stared at my phone in confusion. This was the first form of communication I'd received from Travis in so long, and he seemed excited I was coming over. Was this family really that cruel that they would be excited for my misery?

Well, if that's the case, two can play the game. I quickly got up to take a shower. I was going to look my best tonight. I wasn't going to let Travis and his girl affect me. I was going to be the strong, happy, independent woman I was before the stupid show broke me. And hell, I was going to get my best friend back.

Chapter Thirty

I sat in my car in the Grayson's driveway for twenty minutes before I had the nerve to walk up to the door, where I stood for another ten minutes, debating on what to do. My palms were sweaty, my heart beating too fast, and I was pretty sure I was about to throw up in the bushes.

Why am I doing this?

There had to be an easier way to ease back into the Travis/Riley friendship. This just felt like I was getting thrown into the lion's den. I sucked up my courage and reached out to press the doorbell. Before I could, the door flew open and I was left staring breathlessly at Travis.

"I wasn't sure you were ever going to come in. I saw you sitting in your car thirty minutes ago, I was sure you were going to bolt," Travis said grinning at me as I stepped into the house.

"Yeah, well if I was in my right mind, I would have." I walked farther into the foyer while Travis shut the door behind me. I figured I'd go see if I could help Kathy with dinner, not only to help put myself at ease, but also to get away from this greeting with Travis. I was just about to walk down the hall to the kitchen when I felt Travis grab my wrist and pull me back to his body. My head landed against his chest as he wrapped his arms around me. My entire body tensed under his arms and I struggled to get out of his grip.

"Relax Doll," Travis whispered in my ear. "Let me hug you."

Relax? Was he crazy, we hadn't seen each other in forever and the last time we did see each other, he broke my freaking heart! Yeah, it was a really bad idea to come here tonight. I finally untangled myself from him and took off down the hall without another word. This was not what one would call easing into the situation.

I found Kathy in the kitchen like I thought I would. She was laughing and talking to someone I couldn't see in the corner as I made my way to the island in the middle of the kitchen.

"Hi Kathy, can I help with anything?" I asked coming up next to her and stealing a sliver of green pepper off the cutting board and popping it in my mouth.

"Oh, I think we have it all handled dear," she said, nodding to the corner where the other person had their head in the fridge, before adding the peppers to the salad bowl in front of her. I watched the person in the fridge waiting for her to reveal herself. I hoped it was one of Travis' brothers new girlfriends, and not someone here with Travis. The girl backed out of the fridge, arms loaded with drinks, and turned toward us, allowing me a full view of her face.

Taylor! Oh no. Why are they doing this to me?

"Riley! You're here!" Taylor squealed, setting the drinks on the counter and running over to me pulling me into a hug.

Had I entered the twilight zone? What the hell was going on here? Sure Taylor and I sent texts to each other now and then, and she had been mum about what happened during the finale, but did she really think I was eager to hang out with her when she was Travis' girlfriend? I gave her a small pat on the back, before stepping out of the hug.

"I'm so glad you decided to come! We have so much catching up to do," Taylor said before she went back to the counter to pick up the drinks. "Later, okay?" She quickly exited the kitchen, taking the drinks to the guys in the dining room.

"Kathy…" I started. I was going to tell her that I didn't think this was a good idea, especially now that I knew Taylor was here and clearly the girl Travis chose.

"Oh hush Riley. Enjoy the night. Hang out with your friends. Now go, it's time to eat," she said pushing me out of the kitchen and effectively ending our conversation.

I headed to the dining room, thinking about escaping, but knowing if I did, I'd never hear the end of it. I saw the entire Grayson clan sitting around the table when I entered.

"Riley darling, so happy to have you tonight. It's been too long since we've seen you," Keith said as he wrapped his arms around me, squeezing me into his signature bear hug. I happily hugged him back, relieved to be around someone who didn't have an immediate connection to the show. If ever I needed to know what Travis was going to look like when he got older, I only had to take one look as his father. The two looked exactly alike, aside from Keith's now silver hair and his matured face. Travis even stole his signature grin from his dad, though his dad only used it on Kathy. I was released from his hug, only to be pulled into another one from Travis' brothers, Steve and Chase.

"Little sis, why do you hate us?" Steve asked, pushing Chase away so he could get a full hug from me.

"Um, I didn't know that I did," I said, giving him a quick hug, before pulling a pouting Chase into one.

"But you don't visit anymore. And Travis has been pouting since he got home. You need to do something about that," Chase complained as he released me from the hug.

"Uh…" I started, unsure of what to say.

"I have not been pouting!" Travis yelled from the other end of the table.

"Dude, you sit around listening to sappy love songs and eat ice cream all day. I'd call that pouting," Steve said, laughing as Travis jumped from the chair to try to tackle him. Steve was quick though and escaped Travis, only to hide behind me.

"Don't think Riles will protect you," Travis said, trying to get around me, but every time he would make a move Steve would grip onto me and drag me in that direction.

"Boys, Riley is not a human shield." Keith scolded his sons with a laugh. They ignored him and continued to jerk me around. "Sorry hon." Keith gave me a wink before turning back to his conversation with Taylor and Chase.

"Just admit it, Travis, and no one gets hurt," Steve said, now pulling me back to him and wrapping his arm around my waist like I was his hostage.

"Seriously guys, aren't we a little too old to be playing 'hide behind Riley'?" I asked as I continued to get jerked around. Travis chuckled at me, watching Steve's every move, waiting for the moment to get through.

This was definitely not the first time this had happened to me. His brothers always thought Travis would give up on his pursuit if I was standing in the way. That was never the case, Travis always tried to find a way to get me free and out of the way before he attacked, and if he didn't, well, I got to be in the middle of a Grayson brother sandwich. This time though, I didn't feel like being in that position.

I opened my mouth to yell at the two of them, when Travis saw his chance and grabbed my wrist, pulling me out of Steve's grasp and into his. I hated that butterflies erupted in my stomach when he touched me. Annoyed, I jerked my wrist out of his grasp and walked around the table to sit next to Taylor.

"You two need to grow up," I said rolling my eyes at the two boys who were currently attempting to tackle each other to the floor.

"I'll grow up once he admits he's been pouting for the last two months!" Steve grunted while trying to keep himself in a standing position.

"Not admitting it, because it's not true." Travis breathed heavily straining under his brother's grip.

"You missed Riles, admit it!" Steve fell to his knees panting, but kept his arms around Travis.

Travis paused and let go of Steve, resting back on his heels. "I can admit that. Of course I missed her."

Well if that didn't just get super awkward in two seconds flat.

All eyes turned to me as I ducked my head, grabbing the water glass in front of me and sipping it. Thankfully Kathy came in carrying trays of food, so I didn't have to hide my face for long.

"Boys, get off the floor and help me with the food," she told them, holding the food out for them to place on the table. She didn't even bat an eye at their appearance, as this was a pretty normal occurrence in their house.

Travis and Steve quickly stood up and took the dishes out of their mom's arms, setting them in the middle of the table, family style. Everyone sat down and immediately dug in, mumbling their approval to Kathy as they devoured their food. I glanced up and noticed Travis was sitting directly across from me, staring. I found it odd he wasn't sitting on the other side of his girlfriend, but didn't say anything about it.

Maybe she was already really comfortable with their family. Oh hell, this is probably not her first time here.

How could I have been so naive in thinking Travis wouldn't have brought her here before tonight? They probably spent all summer here for all I knew. I pushed the food around on my plate, no longer hungry, wishing it would be 10 o'clock and I could just go home.

"Well, is everyone done? The show is about to start." Kathy stood up and started gathering the dishes, trying to usher everyone else into the living room.

"I'll help clean up," I said, standing and gathering the dishes in front of me.

"Nonsense, go join them." Kathy tried to take the plates from my hands but I stood firm.

"Please, I just need a break. Please Kathy." I begged her to just let me have this little moment. Kathy nodded and we began the process of putting food away, filling the dishwasher and cleaning up the dining room and kitchen. All too quickly we were done, just as the show was beginning. Kathy physically dragged me into the living room, throwing me down in the only open spot, which of course was next to Travis. Kathy squeezed in on the other side of me, making me slide so close to Travis that our knees were touching. I shifted around uncomfortably, trying to find a way for our bodies to not touch, since it was causing me nothing but panic. Travis noticed my distress and took pity on me, scooting over just a smidge, so there was a quarter inch gap between us.

Well, at least we aren't touching.

I turned my attention to the TV where Travis and the girls were lounging by the pool talking about something or another. I wasn't paying much attention, because my eyes were focused on Nicki draping her body all over Travis. She came off on TV just as she did in real life. I have no idea what people were saying about her, because I stayed away from everything and anything about the show, but I could only imagine no one had nice things to say. I turned my eyes down to my hands and started picking at my nails. There was no way I was going to make it through the night watching this show. Every feeling I'd tried to bury for the last two months had come boiling to the surface and hearing Nicki in the background was almost my undoing.

Can we just get to the end, when he gives the bracelet to Taylor?

I mean, seriously, why was I here anyway? I clearly knew who he picked! So I did what I knew how to do best—I zoned out. Staring at the TV, but not watching and only hearing a buzzing sound in my ears. This was how I was going to get through the night.

I thought I had zoned through the whole show, when Travis bumped my knee with his, bringing me out of the daze.

"You still with us?" he asked, smirking because he knew what I was doing.

"I am now," I groaned, knowing I probably wasn't going to be able to get away with that again and had to actually focus on the show now.

Travis was standing with Nicki on a platform that was placed on the beach. It looked as if Nicki had just gotten there, and clearly tried to make out with Travis, as he was busy rubbing the lipstick off his lips. Finally he got it all wiped off and glared slightly at Nicki who was once again trying to approach him.

"I don't really know what to say to you Nicki, aside from, Riley was right," Travis began, keeping his hands in his pocket and staring Nicki in the eye. She began to pout when he continued, "You are exactly like every other girl I've seen in the past, and quite frankly, I'm tired of that lifestyle." Nicki started to fake sob, but Travis kept his composure.

"Honestly, I never expected to fall in love on this show, but I did," he said giving a far-off smile. My heart dropped hearing those words. He fell in love on the show… he fell in love with Taylor. I sneaked a peek at her, but she was intently watching the TV with a beaming smile on her face.

"This is the point where I would say I just want to be your friend, Nicki, but I can't say that. You have been nothing but rude to the other girls since you've arrived here. You put on a good show when you were around me, but my eyes have been fully open for the last two days. You are not a person I want in my life, friend or otherwise. Bye Nicki, I truly hope you learn to treat others with more respect." Travis began to turn, effectively dismissing Nicki when she screamed causing all of us in the room to jump.

"I will not be dismissed like this Travis. You can't tell me you believe the stories that tramp told you!" Nicki screamed at him. Travis glared back at her. She'd clearly pushed his last button by calling me a tramp.

"No, you're right about that. You shouldn't be leaving now—you should have left the first night, months ago," Travis said just before Nicki's palm connected with his face. Travis laughed and lightly rubbed his cheek, while Nicki was hauled away by two of the crew members, screaming all the way.

"She really was effing crazy!" Travis said to Tessa who had just joined him. Tessa smiled and nodded but said nothing, before it cut to a commercial break.

I stared at Travis in shock. I could not believe he had said that to Nicki on national television. I mean, don't get me wrong, I wanted to give him a high five and applaud him for doing what I had been trying to do, but I was shocked he would pick her to go to the finale, only to demolish her like that.

"I should have listened to you Riles," Travis said shrugging when he noticed my stare.

"I...that...um..." I couldn't form a full sentence. I wanted to tell him that was amazing, but the words got caught in my throat when I saw Taylor over his shoulder grinning at us. I was ready to smack the smile right off her face. I turned back to the TV, pretending to be enthralled in the commercials while everyone else chattered on about Nicki's dismissal. When Travis appeared back on the TV, everyone quieted down and turned their attention back to the show.

"Well Travis are you ready to tell your decision to Taylor?" Tessa asked as she set a box containing the final bracelet on the podium next to him.

"I cannot wait!" Travis replied excitedly. He tugged at the sleeves of his shirt and stared nervously down the beach where Taylor would come from.

The screen cut to Taylor walking down the beach in a flowery summer dress. She looked gorgeous with her hair pulled off to the side in a low ponytail, the dress floated around her from the breeze off the lake, and she wore the most dazzling smile—much like the one she wore earlier tonight.

"Taylor." Travis breathed out her name as she approached him.

"Hi Travis." Taylor giggled slightly as Travis pulled her into his arms.

Oh God, I can't watch this!

I was starting to squirm in my seat, sitting here with Travis and Taylor in the room was completely uncomfortable. And I could feel all eyes turn to me to watch my reaction to this.

Seriously, I need to leave.

I was about to stand up, when Kathy clamped her hand down on my knee.

"I know this hurts, but you need to watch it," Kathy said quietly so no one could overhear.

"You guys are evil. Horrible, evil human beings," I muttered to her, hoping to get some reaction out of her, all I got was a laugh.

"I'm sure it seems that way honey. Just watch," she said nodding towards the TV. I turned my attention back to the TV, hearing the end of what Travis was saying to Taylor.

"...glad we've become so close." He was telling her while holding her hands in his. "I want you to know I value the friendship we have made here." Taylor nodded, continuing to dazzle us with her smile.

"Like I told Nicki, I never expected to fall in love on this show. Heck, when my mom mentioned me falling in love before the show even started, I laughed at her," he continued. The room around me chuckled, as I remembered Travis and Kathy's conversation in the hospital those many months ago. "But I did. I managed to fall in love in the most unexpected place with the most unexpected girl."

I felt a tear drop down my cheek. My heart was breaking all over again. Watching this was worse than if I had watched my own elimination, I was sure of it.

"I hope you know where I'm going with this," Travis said to Taylor on the TV.

Taylor smiled up at him, before pulling him into a hug. "Of course I do," she whispered, hugging him tightly. Travis wrapped his arms around her and they stood frozen like that for what felt like hours, until Taylor finally pulled back.

"You're pretty special, you know that?" he said to her with an awed expression.

"I value my friendships more than anything," she said with a laugh. "Goodbye Travis." She squeezed his hand, before turning to walk away.

I blinked, more tears dropping down my face.

What the hell?!

Taylor was walking away from Travis and they were both grinning like idiots on the television.

Taylor stopped and turned around. "Hey Travis," she called back to him.

Okay, this was the moment they all laugh and say 'just kidding!' and she goes running back into his arms. It must be some sick inside joke of theirs.

"Let your brothers know I'm single!" she yelled, before she turned around and ran up the steps to the house. Travis let out a deep, full laugh, wiping his eyes on his shirt as Tessa approached.

"Well Travis. I can say this is not how anyone envisioned the show ending. Want to tell us what's going on?" she asked curiously. Apparently no one but Travis and Taylor had known what was going to happen.

"Like I said, I fell in love on this show, with the most amazing, caring, adventurous… stubborn girl I've ever met. Little did I know it was going to be with the girl I've known since I was ten. The girl I've spent more time with than anyone else in this world. The girl I am hoping is still waiting for me when I get home. I fell in love with my best friend, Tessa, and now I have to go get her back." The screen went black, before the credits and a TV promo aired.

I was pretty sure I was bawling now, unable to look away from the TV.

What the hell is going on?

Slowly I took in the rest of the room; everyone was staring at me, watching my reaction. I turned to Travis and just stared. I was going to ask him what the hell was going on and how he could have broken my heart like he did. And that's when I saw it. Taylor had been sitting next to Chase the whole night, and he had his arm draped around her, holding her close. She smiled reassuringly at me and leaned back into Chase.

"What the hell?!" I screamed before standing and running out the nearest door I could see, which happened to take me into the backyard.

Chapter Thirty One

I ran to the end of the yard where a few canopy swings sat circling a fire pit. I fell down on one of the swings, breathing heavily with tears still streaming down my face.

Did Travis just choose me?

I was so confused. Why the hell would he break my heart only days before the finale, only to walk away with no one at the end, intent on 'getting me back'? This made absolutely no sense and if he thought he was just going to say a few sweet words on national TV and I was going to fall into his arms, he was out of his freaking mind. I heard feet slowly crunch through the grass towards me, until they stopped right in front of me. My eyes were down, so I was able to see Travis' shoes before he spoke.

"Riles, please let me explain." His voice was strong and rehearsed, which just pissed me off even more.

"You want to explain? You're really going to have the right words to tell me why on Earth you would break my heart, not talk to me for two months and then tell the entire nation you are in love with me? You are really going to explain that?" I screamed at him, standing to face him. I was not going to back down on this. I had been living with a completely broken heart for two months when it wasn't even necessary. I had been bored out of my mind, not being able to work because they thought it would be awkward for me to be around Travis. He had cut me off from everyone I ever cared about all because of what? TV show ratings?

OMG, was that what this was about? Ratings?!

"Shit Travis. Please don't tell me this was to get ratings. Please don't tell me Jim put you up to this, so everyone would talk about the end of this season and they'd have a lock for season two." I begged him as I grabbed his shirt shaking him slightly.

"Riles, calm down," he said gently, lightly touching my hands where they gripped his shirt, and pulling them off. He led me over to the swing I had vacated when he came out and sat down, still holding my hand. I fell into place next to him, tucking my legs under me.

"Travis, tell me it wasn't for the ratings." I begged him once more. I could never get over my broken heart if that was why he did it.

"Of course it wasn't about the ratings. Do you think I care about them?" he said while shaking his head.

"Then… what the hell Trav?" I couldn't help it, I needed to know why he did all this. Travis didn't say anything for a while as he stared at my hands in his.

"You're still wearing them," Travis said, trailing his hand down the bracelets on my wrist smiling. I winced as he touched them, feeling silly I had kept them on.

"I like the way they look," I said weakly. It even sounded like a lame excuse to me. The truth was, I'd tried to take them off countless times, but each time I started pulling them from my wrist my hand froze and my heart thumped loudly. It was silly, but they felt like the only connection I had left to Travis. And yes, I did like the way they looked, it was like they were made for me.

"Can I explain now? Everything?" Travis asked, resting my hand on his lap. He turned so he was looking directly at me. I nodded my head, knowing if I opened my mouth, I would probably talk him out of saying anything. And I really wanted to know what he was thinking.

He took a deep breath and began, "I never meant for things to turn out how they did. If you told me I was going to fall in love with my best friend, I would have said you were crazy. I've known you forever, Doll. I can't say I've never thought of us together before, but it wasn't on my radar when I signed on for the show." He was telling me things I already knew, and I was about to call him on it when he continued.

"I know you didn't want to be there. I know you did it all for me. You dealt with the girls like a champ and got all up in my face when I wouldn't listen to you." He chuckled, recalling the memories. "I definitely know you did not sign up to actually be in the running. We had a deal and I broke it. I fell for you and I wasn't ready to let you go." He paused and took a deep breath.

"I can't tell you exactly when I knew I wanted you to stay on as more than my best friend. But being surrounded by all those girls vying for my attention, *you* were the one who stood out. You knew me, you didn't put up a front around me, you were always yourself. When we had our first argument over a bunch of petty girls and you didn't show up at my place when I asked you to—that's when I knew. That is when I knew I couldn't live without you, and the past fifteen years of pent up emotions hit me hard." He paused, gripping my hand tightly. "I knew your birthday would be the best time to show you what you mean to me, so I went all out. Bought you a dress I knew you'd never choose, rented out Al's so we wouldn't be interrupted, ordered Chinese for dinner and had the best bakery in the city make you a cake. I wanted it to be a day you'd remember forever—the day we stepped into our future together." Tears started rolling down my cheeks again as I listened on.

"When you kissed me back, my heart felt ready to explode. I never thought I would feel the way I did. I was so effing happy you were willing to go there with me. That night, when you were acting all weird at my place, I thought I had pushed you too far and I was losing you. But that wasn't the case, was it?" He grinned slyly at me. "Anyway, you know the rest. I had never been happier. It sucked that I still had this television show I needed to finish, but I knew I could act my way through it. What I didn't take into consideration was how you'd feel about it. I never knew you to be jealous, so it floored me when I saw it coming from you. I tried to reassure you over and over again that you had nothing to worry about, but you wouldn't believe me. And watching back through those episodes, I can see why. I'm apparently a better actor than I thought." He laughed, staring off into the distance.

"You were acting? What about the kiss with Nicki? That didn't look like acting!" I screamed at him, pulling my hands from his grasp. Just remembering that was breaking my heart all over again.

Travis leaned close to me and lifted my chin with his finger so I was looking him in the eye. "What you saw and what actually happened are two different things." He never broke eye contact with me, but I couldn't help rolling my eyes.

"Trav, I know what I saw. It never looked like you pulled back or tried to stop it."

"But you never *heard* what I told her. When she kissed me the first time, I was shocked and I did step out of it. To be honest, I was pretty pissed she had even done that. Just before she attacked, we were talking about you and how I felt towards you." He tugged my hands back into his.

Well…that's a surprise.

"I saw her wicked grin and I knew she was going to do it again, so I grabbed her face to stop her. I told her it would never happen again. She may have surprised me once, but I wouldn't let her take any more from me. Then I reiterated that I loved *you*. And even though the show was still going on, there was no other choice. It was always going to be you, Riles."

"But, there was another kiss." I pointed out.

Travis sighed and continued. "Yes. I made the mistake of loosening my hold on her face and she launched. She was bound and determined to make me forget about you—and now I know she also planned the whole thing because she knew you could see us. I'm pretty sure you must not have seen the whole thing because as soon as she kissed me, I gripped her arms and pulled her off me. It took everything in me to not shake her for what she was doing. I told her she could keep trying that all night, but I would never change my mind. I would never choose her. She just threw her head back with a laugh and said she would take me up on that. I just let go of her and walked to the other side of the blanket making sure there was distance between us for the rest of the date. I'm pretty sure Jim knew I was almost at my breaking point with her, because he made sure to position some cameras directly between us so she couldn't try it again."

All I could do was stare into his eyes, my mind wandering back to that day and what I had seen. His explanation did make sense. I obviously couldn't have heard anything he had said and my mind had reacted to only what I saw.

Crap, I overreacted about the whole thing and never let him explain.

"Well…I feel like an idiot now," I mumbled looking back at our hands tangled together.

"But you're not one. Anyone would come to the same conclusion you did…they just probably would have let me explain then, instead of two months down the road. Or they would have watched the show and saw it all play out on there. Obviously you never watched a single episode." Travis smiled at me, clearly knowing the answer.

I shook my head. "The only episode I watched was the one tonight."

"Figured as much."

"Okay, that explains one thing. But why eliminate me from the show?" That was the one question I needed the answer to most.

"Riles, I felt us breaking. I felt this show tearing us apart and I couldn't let that happen. So when you reminded me that you never signed up for the show and were tired of dealing with the drama of the game, I decided I needed to do something rash. You said you were done playing the game. I was so afraid that meant you were done with us, but you said you wanted me, that was all. So I made a decision the best decision for you—I let you go." He stared at me as I swallowed the lump in my throat.

"The best decision for me? You broke my heart, Trav!" I wailed, unable to keep my emotions in check. Travis pulled me into a hug and I went willingly. He held me close, rubbing his hand up and down my back.

"Do you have any idea how much it broke me?" he asked softly. I remembered back to when I left the show, seeing Travis crumble on the stoop with the look of agony on his face. I hadn't let him explain any of this before I left. I never considered he'd have a broken heart too.

I wiped at my face with my sleeve and cleared my throat, "Why let me go though? You could have kicked Nicki out and none of this would have happened."

"I thought of that. I did. But I didn't want our relationship to start off that way—me picking you off some dating show. I wanted to do it away from all the cameras and prying eyes. I figured since you hated the show, that's how you would want it too," he said as I choked on a sob. "I kept telling you it was always you. When are you going to learn to trust me?" He chuckled, pulling me back into another hug. I gripped his shoulders, holding him close to me, hoping to make up for lost time.

"I'm a girl. I have weird emotions." I sniffed into his shoulder and his body rumbled with laughter. Another question was still nagging in the back of my head. "So, why didn't you talk to me for the last two months?" I asked into his sleeve.

Travis sighed into my hair. "We knew there were going to be reporters swarming. We obviously couldn't give away the ending of the show, since it hadn't aired yet, but reporters were getting rumors of who the final two were. Jim decided it was best for Taylor to be seen around town and with me to try to give it away that she was the one I chose. Since the ending of the show was something no one would expect, Jim decided using Taylor as a decoy was for the best. And since we were all still under contract with the show, we had no choice."

"And Taylor was okay with this?" I asked, unable to believe she would just do this out of the goodness of her heart.

"Taylor jumped at the chance. Apparently you mentioned I had brothers." Travis laughed into my hair.

"Seriously? Taylor really came for your brothers?!" That was so unexpected I couldn't help but laugh.

"Well, during our last date we had a night…alone. Typically it would be the time the couples, uh, get to know each other." Travis blushed. "But clearly that was not happening. So Taylor and I just talked and she ended up badgering me about my brothers. Taylor acts all shy and quiet, but she can be very demanding! So long story short, by the end of the night she had Chase's number and they were already texting like high schoolers."

"But what about what she said at the end of the show tonight? 'Let your brothers know I'm single.' What was that about?" I wasn't sure if my brain could take any more puzzles.

"She was just throwing it out for effect. I'm pretty sure her and Chase had stayed up all night talking, so he clearly knew just how single she was."

"Why did you never text me more than a few generic words?" There had to be a better reason why we had almost no communication at all.

"Do you know how hard it was for me to stay away from you? To not run over to your house, scoop you up in my arms, kiss you like crazy and never let you go? I wanted to call you about twenty times a day and always had the urge to text you every other minute. But I had to stay away. Completely. Otherwise this ending would have been ruined," Travis said, pulling me tighter against his chest.

"Travis Grayson, you are the strangest, most confusing man I've ever met."

"You said you'd wait for me. Is that still the truth?" He pulled back, staring deeply into my eyes, his twinkling with joy.

"Trav, you put Nicki in her place on national TV, you hooked my best girl friend up with your brother, and you created this crazy plan because you thought that's what I wanted." I shook my head at him. "You did this all for me?"

Travis gave me his sexy grin and nodded. "What can I say? You're the girl for me, Doll."

"You suck, you know that right?" I said, slapping at his arm.

He laughed his beautiful full belly laugh and pulled me into his arms. "So Riles, it's now or never? What do you choose?"

"I choose us," I said, trailing my hand across his cheekbone, before reaching my mouth up to his and capturing his lips in mine.

Epilogue (One Year Later)

I stood at the top of the hill with Travis, looking over the scores of the other riders.

"You don't even have to do this run Trav, you'll still win the gold," I said, hoping he'd play it safe and not throw any big tricks that could land him in the hospital…again.

"Riles, I still have to do my run," he complained, having said it numerous times in the past.

"A victory run?" That meant the most basic tricks and him just pumping his fist in the air.

"Yes Riles, a victory run." He rolled his eyes at me as catcalls started coming from behind him.

"Someone is whipped!" One of the riders called to him, making a whipping sound.

"Someone grew up and has another person to look out for." Travis turned to them and held up my hand, flashing the diamond ring on my finger. I pulled my hand out of his grip and smacked his shoulder as the other rider shrugged and walked away.

"Would you stop showing the ring off to everyone?" He had done it every day for the last month since he asked me to marry him.

"What can I say? I'm freaking happier than hell you agreed to spend the rest of your life with me." He smirked at me and laughed as I swatted at him again.

"Well, what else was I going to do with my life? I'm still your assistant. I'd still have to be with you every single day.

Might as well make it more beneficial for me." I winked at him and ran my hands up and down his chest.

"Riley Logan, are you trying to seduce me?"

"Is it working?" I asked wickedly. Maybe if I kept it up, he'd just throw his final round and I wouldn't have to worry about him like usual.

"Not a chance. I know your ways." He laughed and stepped away from me.

"You guys are more nauseating than usual," Chase said coming up behind Travis with Taylor at his side.

"Oh hush, they are the cutest couple I know!" Taylor said and slapped Chase in the chest.

"What the hell does that make us?" He tried to sound wounded.

"Beauty and the Beast?" Travis shot out with a laugh. Chase broke free from Taylor and launched himself on his brother. They proceeded to fall on the ground and started rolling around in the dirt.

"I don't know why we put up with them." Taylor laughed as she walked over to me.

"Probably because we took pity on them when no other girl would." I bumped her shoulder with mine as we watched the boys wrestle for a few minutes.

"You boys are going to be the death of me," Kathy said from behind them. "Get up, both of you. Act like I raised you to act."

"I thought that's what we were doing," Chase said, dodging his mother's arm as it came out to smack the back of his head.

"I think it's time to go back to our spots. Good luck Travis," Taylor called over her shoulder as she pulled Chase down the side of the hill.

"So Travis, I wanted to talk to you about the TV offer…" Kathy started as she was brushing dirt off her son.

"NO!" Travis and I both yelled at the same time. The producers of *Xtreme Bachelor* had two successful seasons following Travis' season. When they caught wind Travis had proposed, they had been calling non-stop with offers of a TV show, detailing our lives as we planned our wedding and airing the wedding itself live. When Kathy brought it to our attention, I'd thought she was joking. Why would she ever think that would be okay with us? But she kept pushing and pushing, trying to get us to agree to something. She had gotten the offer down to just airing the wedding, but Travis and I'd had enough of reality TV for the rest of our lives.

"I wish you would think about it," Kathy complained, looking at her phone and typing out a quick message, presumably to Jim.

"Mom, a reality show almost tore Riles and I apart. That will never happen again," Travis told Kathy as seriously as he could. Hopefully this time she would understand we were serious.

"Okay, okay. I get it. But I was right the first time around," she muttered, still typing away on her phone.

"What are you talking about?" I asked.

"You two were obviously not going to take the chance on each other unless something dramatic happened. I knew you were perfect for each other, so when Jim called about the show, I knew Riley had to be on it too," Kathy said, finally looking up at the two of us.

Travis and I stared dumbfounded at his mom. I was unable to believe she put us through that whole show just because she wanted us to be together. There had to have been an easier way.

"You can thank me later." She patted Travis on the head, before heading down by Chase and Taylor.

"Your mom may be a ninja," I said as Travis turned back to me. "She's the sneakiest person I know." Travis laughed and slung his arm around my shoulder.

We watched the next few riders in silence, until it was time for Travis' victory lap. The crowd was cheering loudly since they knew Travis was next and that he had the gold medal locked. The whole world fell away as Travis turned to face me, holding on to my arms.

"I love you, Riles," Travis whispered to me as he pulled me into a hug. I don't think I'd ever get used to him saying those words to me. My stinking heart still beat too fast whenever I was around him and those butterflies never went away.

"I love you, Trav," I said pressing my lips to his, giving him a quick, sweet kiss. He pressed his forehead to mine and we stayed that way until his name was called. He gave me a chaste kiss before he started to pull out of the hug.

"Be calm. Be cool. Be safe," I whispered to him before I released him from my arms.

Travis gave me his sexy grin and nodded. "Always, Doll."

**Riley and Travis' story continues
in the short story**

Forever Us

Two years ago, Riley Logan agreed to go on a reality dating
show with her best friend, Travis Grayson.
She didn't expect to fall in love with him.
One year ago, Travis asked Riley to marry him.
She said yes.
Now in the days building up to the wedding Riley and Travis
navigate through the finishing touches.
A bachelorette party Riley is sure to never forget.
And the day they finally become - Forever Us.

This is a short story, a little over 11,000 words.

Also Available by Caylie Marcoe

Parting Chances

A Note About Reviews

If you enjoyed this book, please consider writing a review on Amazon and/or Goodreads. Every single review helps, even if it's only a sentence or two. Thank you so much for reading!

Acknowledgments

Chris—Thank you for dealing with a messy house, eating many frozen pizzas, and putting up with me using the computer all.the.time. Your love and support mean the world to me.

Lilly and Josh—Thank you for loving frozen pizza, mac and cheese and pb&j. For being content watching PBS in the mornings and letting Mommy type up a chapter or two. And for being my 'writing buddies' throughout this process.

Hales—Oh jeez. Thank you for thinking the first chapter was good enough to turn into a full length novel. For reading each chapter as I wrote them. For letting me bounce ideas off you and not getting upset when I gave away a spoiler. For being there whenever I needed to complain, vent, laugh, cry…you name it…you were there. For listening to those podcasts and reading those books to have the best knowledge of self publishing, so you could answer any of my questions. Seriously…just thank you for being the best freaking friend a girl could ask for!

Rebel Writers—You guys!! I don't know what I would have done without you. Your support, feedback and advice have kept me going. When a few of you finished your novels, that was the push I needed to finish this one. Thank you, for not only being great peers, but for becoming great friends.

Theresa—You are amazeballs! Your edits made this book so.much.better. Thank you for all the time you spent on this bad boy!

Steff—Thank you for offering to edit the very first draft. For letting me harass you with questions and just letting me talk through ideas with you.

Lisa—Thank you for dealing with my crazy obsessive ideas for the cover. For never complaining when I asked you to change the background, font, positioning, color... And for not throwing me off a cliff when in the end I decided to just go with the original picture you worked on. I love this cover so much and promise to not be a creative design freak for the next one!

My beta readers—Kathryn, Leigh and Lenore (along with Hales and Lisa and the Rebel Writers), you ladies have NO idea how great you are! You gave me such amazing feedback and edits! I thought I had a good book before you read it, but you made it *great!* Thank you a million times over!!

Rachel—Thank you for helping me perfect the blurb. For giving me advice on the other side of being an author. For being there whenever I had a question... and for writing such amazing novels!

Anyone who has ever told me I could/should write a book—Your words stuck with me more than you will know! Thank you for believing in me!

YOU—Thank you for picking up this book and giving it a chance! Whether you loved it or hated it—*thank you* for reading it! It means the world to me.

About the Author

Born and raised in the frozen tundra of Wisconsin, Caylie fell in love with reading at a young age. With her lively imagination, she created numerous stories in her head throughout her childhood and teenage years. Finally at 16 she sat down at the computer and wrote out her first full length novel. That pacified her for a time. However, the stories kept swimming through her mind. In 2013 she typed out Chapter One of three different novels and sent them off to a close friend for review. At her friends advice, she started working on Choose Us.

When she isn't slaving away at the keyboard, Caylie is an avid reader, and lover of coffee... copious amounts of coffee. She also has an unhealthy addiction to tv shows—binge watching is her favorite.

She chases her two kids around the house all day, and has a husband whom she adores.

And I love interacting with my readers! Feel free to message me or Facebook me to talk about the book, ask question, or chat about...anything! I'm game for it all. You guys are awesome! I can be found online at:

Blog & Website:
www.authorcayliemarcoe.com
Facebook:
www.facebook.com/CaylieMarcoeAuthor
Twitter:
@authorcayliem
Instagram:
@cayliemarcoe